Pulse

Landry Family Security
Book 1

Adriana Locke

Paperback ISBN: 978-1-960355-27-0

Cover Design: Kari March, www.karimarch.com
Photographer: Michelle Lancaster, @lanefotograf
Editor: Marion Archer, Marion Making Manuscripts
Editor: Jenny Sims, Editing 4 Indies
Proofreader: Michele Ficht

To Atlee,
You worked hard for this.

Books by Adriana Locke

My Amazon Store
Signed Copies

Brewer Family Series
The Proposal | The Arrangement

Carmichael Family Series
Flirt | Fling | Fluke | Flaunt | Flame

Landry Family Series
Sway | Swing | Switch | Swear | Swink | Sweet

Landry Family Security Series
Pulse

Gibson Boys Series
Crank | Craft | Cross | Crave | Crazy

The Mason Family Series
Restraint | The Relationship Pact | Reputation | Reckless | Relentless | Resolution

The Marshall Family Series
More Than I Could | This Much Is True

The Exception Series
The Exception | The Perception

For a complete reading order and more information, visit www.adrianalocke.com.

Synopsis

USA Today bestselling author Adriana Locke delivers a spicy, age-gap, grumpy sunshine, workplace romance in the first book in the brand-new Landry Security series.

Troy Castelli acts like it's my fault that we're cooped up in a room with one bed overlooking the ocean. I didn't ask for a stalker to break into my house and then send me a threatening email detailing my demise. And I sure as heck didn't request that my boss send Troy and his uber-elite bodyguard skills to accompany me out of town—although I'm not mad about it.

A paid tropical vacation with a grumpy, gray-eyed bad boy in a suit isn't exactly a burden.

But it is a giant test of my willpower.

Troy's alpha protector tendencies drive me wild. His arrogant smirk gets under my skin. But it's his not-so-innocent touches, heated looks, and touch-her-and-die vibes that are the final strike that ignite our explosive chemistry.

The longer we're together, the more his broody exterior slips, and I get a glimpse of the real man beneath the sculpted muscles. I'm determined not only to unearth his mysterious past but also to make him realize what we have is more than just a fling in paradise.

That is, unless my stalker gets me first.

Chapter One

T roy

"You don't need a parachute to skydive. You only need a parachute to skydive *twice*." Lincoln Landry smirks over the rim of his coffee mug, quite pleased with himself.

But really, when is he not?

I run a hand across my forehead, lamenting my decision not to work from home today. I could be in my sweats at my desk in the guest room, eating buttery cinnamon toast—alone. Instead, I'm here with this guy.

"It's too early for this shit," I say.

"Come on, Castelli. You have to admit that I'm onto something here."

"All you're onto, *Landry*, is proving you need a hobby."

"I have plenty of hobbies."

"He's not lying," Ford Landry says, coming into my office and closing the door behind him. He takes a seat across from me beside his brother.

Morning sunlight streams through my office windows, filling the

1

space with a warm glow. The cloudless sky is the perfect shade of blue, and birds chirp just outside the glass. The day held so much promise until Lincoln walked in twenty minutes ago.

"Your wife just called," Ford tells his brother.

Lincoln bristles. "Why is my wife calling *you*?"

"Because it seems that you bought me a new golf club for my birthday, but Danielle found it in the garage this morning. She wanted me to know she'd take it to Ellie this afternoon."

"Dammit," Lincoln groans, shaking his head. "How did she find it?"

"One of your kids lost a ball, and she was looking for it." Ford grins. "Found the club instead."

I rock back in my desk chair. "Something tells me that club isn't Ford's."

"Hell no, it's not Ford's," Lincoln says, glancing over his shoulder. "No offense."

"None taken," Ford says, laughing. "How could I be offended when I'm going to get so much entertainment watching Danielle fuck with you over this?"

"She was just on my case about how my sports equipment is taking over the garage and made me promise I wouldn't buy anything else until I sorted everything I already owned. But then I saw an ad for a titanium driver. The moment I saw that beautiful shaft, I knew I had to have it. Even the screws are sexy."

"Good thing, because it sounds like that screw is all the screwing you'll be getting for a while," Ford says.

"Maybe, but it was worth it. I can imagine that shaft—"

I laugh. "Sounds like a personal problem to me."

Ford stretches his legs out in front of him, clearly amused. "So you decided to tell her it was a gift for me?"

"She saw the purchase on the credit card bill. I panicked. I was thinking on my feet."

I snort. "Well, we know that never works well for you."

"What doesn't work well for me? Thinking on my feet?" Lincoln asks.

"Thinking on your feet isn't your problem. Thinking at all is usually a struggle for you, though."

Ford chuckles, much to his brother's dismay. Lincoln rolls his eyes and turns his attention to his phone. Ford motions for me to give him a minute while he, too, checks his device.

I shuffle through the stack of papers I gathered before Lincoln's grand entrance and arrange them in order of importance. The only sound aside from the birds outside is Lincoln's fingertips frenziedly tapping out texts, presumably to his wife.

Danielle won't be pissed. Not for long, anyway. In the fifteen-ish years I've known Lincoln—since the day I left the military and Ford's family offered me a job—I've realized no one can stay mad at him long.

Not even me—and sometimes I try.

"Looks like you need to strap on that second parachute and head home," I say, winking at Lincoln when he looks up.

He narrows his eyes, but his frustration melts away into laughter. "I can't even be pissed at you. Well done."

"What did I miss?" Ford asks.

"I was trying to explain to him that he needs to get a life," Lincoln says. "He needs to try new things. Live a little."

I start to fire back that I have a life—one that I like a whole damn lot—but my phone buzzes in front of me. When I see the name, I swipe it off my desk.

"Excuse me for a second," I say, unlocking the screen. A ghost of a smile tugs at my lips as I read the message.

> Dahlia: Good morning, sunshine! I saw your truck in the parking lot. First, learn how to park. You're supposed to stay between the lines, not have the back end halfway into the other parking spot. Don't drive a big truck if you can't control it. Second, can you swing by and see me before you leave?

Ford and Lincoln's conversation fades into the background.

> Me: No.

I imagine my assistant's freckles pulling together across the bridge of her cute little button nose and the gasp she probably hissed in exasperation when she read my two-lettered response. Amusement settles against my lips.

> Dahlia: <frustrated emoji> Let's not start the week off like this.

I don't respond. Instead, I fight a smile and watch for the flurry of texts I know are coming.

Three ... two ... one ...

She never fails.

> Dahlia: I need your reports from last week.
>
> Dahlia: And a copy of your new driver's license.
>
> Dahlia: You DID get your license renewed, didn't you? <worried emoji>

> Dahlia: I set a reminder on your calendar on Friday. You can't just ignore my reminders!

> Dahlia: DAMMIT, TROY. DON'T IGNORE ME

> Dahlia: I hope Lincoln is in your office and he's driving you batshit crazy.

My tongue runs along my bottom lip as I grin.

> Dahlia: My grandma always said not to use the word hate because it was too powerful, but if I could guarantee she wasn't turning over in her grave, I'd pop it right into this conversation. Instead— I HEAVILY dislike you right now.

> Me: What's new?

> Dahlia: <crying emoji> Why do you do this to me?

Because it's so much fun.

"Everything okay?" Ford asks.

"Yeah." I set my phone down. "Sorry about that."

Ford gives me a curious look, but Lincoln smirks. *Asshole.*

"Although the parachute analogy was rough," Ford says, "I'm going to use it as a jumping-off point."

"No pun intended," Lincoln says.

"That doesn't make sense, Lincoln," I say.

"Yes, it does. He's using the parachute as a jumping-off point. Like you'd jump out of a plane. Get it?"

I shake my head. "No. I don't. But let's move on." I turn my attention back to Ford. "What are we jumping into?"

He shifts in his seat. Instinctively, I move in mine.

There isn't a thing in the world that I wouldn't do for Ford. I owe him everything—most of all, my loyalty. But I know him well enough to know when he's about to say something he knows I won't like.

Like now.

Ford clears his throat. "I'm sending Calvin to Los Angeles to handle the Clementine project."

"*What?*"

"I know." He sighs. "Don't be mad."

A slow chill snakes down my spine. *Take a deep breath, Castelli.*

"Don't be mad? I'm not mad," I say. "Because I know you're going to tell me you have a new client that you need me to handle, and I'm fine with that. Not a problem."

Lincoln frowns.

"You do have a choice." Ford eyes me warily.

"Everybody has choices. Just like you have one right now."

I stare at him, trying to cut through our professional relationship and hit him in the *we were friends in a combat zone* friendship. It might come across a little more aggressive than I intend. Lucky for Ford, or for me since he *is* the boss, he doesn't call me out on it.

"Let's remember I don't have a say in anything," Lincoln says, holding his hands at his chest in defense. "I'm just here."

I turn to him and lift a brow. "Why *are* you here exactly?"

"Moral support."

"Moral support?" Ford asks. "I'm giving Troy a choice of assignments, not firing him. He doesn't need your moral support."

Lincoln scoffs. "You're the one who said Troy was going to be pissed. Maybe I'm here to offer *you* moral support in case he decides to use his particular skill set to force your hand."

Ford volleys back at him, getting a quick retort from Lincoln. I glance at my phone.

Dahlia: Are you coming to see me or not?

Dahlia: Theo came by to see me, and I don't even work directly with him.

> Dahlia: I'm glad someone likes me.

> Dahlia: Maybe I'll ask Becca if she wants to trade—you for Theo.

I chuckle under my breath, my fingers flying across the screen. I stop myself and read through the text before I hit send. *Thank God.*

> Me: Tell Theo to go fuck himself and to stay out of your office.

I backspace over the words and exhale sharply, hoping my cheeks aren't as flushed as I think they are.

Dahlia Lovelace makes me come unglued. She's everything that gets under my skin. She's habitually late. She pokes every button she can find to irritate me. The woman is always fucking happy.

And she's wildly intelligent, capable of anything, and so damn beautiful that I can't see straight.

Working alongside her for the past two years has been a bigger challenge than trying to keep the world's biggest pop star safe. I remind myself daily that she's forbidden—*untouchable.* Even if crossing the line with my assistant wasn't completely unprofessional, I couldn't do that to her. Not with the shit I carry.

I wouldn't do that to my worst enemy.

> Dahlia: Don't make it hard, Troy. <winking emoji>

I imagine her kissable pout pressed together in a cheeky grin as she typed those words. *Don't make it hard? Too late.*

"So what are my options?" I ask as if I hadn't checked out of our conversation for a minute *and* as if I don't already know the answer. "Let's get this over with."

Ford's jaw sets, bracing for impact. "Your first choice is to work with Laina Kelley's team for another six weeks."

I knew it. "I don't understand why I have to contend with all of that pop star bullshit every fucking time."

"Because she specifically requests *you*," Ford says. "She thinks you're a hero."

"*Come on.* I gave her a ride when she fled her wedding—something I was paid to do, by the way. It's hardly heroic."

Ford's look reminds me I didn't *just* drive her away from the church. I also defused a situation with her movie star ex, physically removed her asshole father from her property, and took a bullet for her—thank God for bulletproof vests—last month.

"You know, there are people who call me a hero, too." Lincoln nods proudly. "Sometimes, you just have to take the compliment."

I fold my hands on the table over my phone. It buzzes against my palms with an incoming text that I have to ignore. "Of course, you know what I mean. Saving lives and saving home runs from center field. Same thing."

"I know you don't love this option," Ford says, ignoring my stab at his brother.

"Ford, I'd almost rather be assigned to Lincoln's security team—"

"Hey!"

"—than to have to go back to Laina's," I continue. "She's not the problem. She's great, and I really like her husband. He's good shit. But every time she walks outside a building, there's so much screaming, crying, and ... *goofiness.*" I sigh at the thought of contending with that again. "What about Ezra? He'd be great. He loves that atmosphere."

"Ezra is the lead on Graham's team now," Ford says.

"No one's going after our brother," Lincoln says, snorting. "G would bore them to death. He's his own personal defense system. Just tell him to start talking if someone comes at him. They'll leave after two sentences. Tell him to talk fast, and he's golden."

As much as I don't want to laugh at Lincoln and feed his ego, I do.

"Fine." Ford shrugs. "I can call Sebastian back from his post with the Abbotts as their travels will be over and they'll return to normal detail. Laina is comfortable with Sebastian. But if I do that, you're taking option two."

"Which is ..."

"You're taking a vacation."

I stare at him, unblinking. "Is that why you sent Lincoln here this morning to discuss living life with parachutes—to try to set the stage somehow?"

Ford lifts a brow. "Do you really think I'd send Lincoln here to butter you up?"

"Yeah, good point." I push back into my chair. "I don't need a vacation, Ford."

"You haven't taken time off in years," Ford says. "I'm starting to worry about you. Everyone needs a break."

"Not me. Vacations mean sitting around and doing nothing. That means too much time on my hands to think and ruminate about life."

And if anyone should understand that, it's you, Ford. We exchange a silent look that only the two of us understand.

"Atlas comes off Laina's detail on Monday," Ford says. "You have until Friday to decide whether you're going to Nashville with her team or on vacation." He levels his gaze with mine. "I need you healthy, man. Please consider the vacation."

My breathing grows shallow, and the room stills.

This has been a recurring conversation over the past eighteen months, and I've managed to weasel my way out of it each time. But I've known this day was coming—when Ford takes a hard stand. And now, here we are.

Once Ford and I retired from the military, the only thing that kept my life from falling apart was the opportunities the Landrys gave me. They took me from my lowest point to ... this.

I never imagined that I'd be driving around fancy cars carrying Ford's brother to events as the governor of Georgia. Who was I to be wearing expensive suits day in and day out? How did I manage to be the right-hand man to the premiere security company in the United States?

That all happened because of Ford. He saved my life, both in and out of the military. And for that, I'll always be there for him ... even if it means taking jobs I don't love.

"I have a couple of meetings today," Ford says, standing. Lincoln gets to his feet, too. "Want to ride with me? We can get some lunch on the way back."

"Can I come?" Lincoln asks. "I don't want to go home yet."

Ford's shoulder bumps his brother.

"Sure," I say. "Let me take care of a few things in here first."

"Not a problem. I have a couple of things to do, anyway." He opens the door but turns back to me. "Oh—*hey*. One more thing."

"Yeah?"

"Stop in and see Dahlia. She said she thought your phone might be dead this morning." Ford grins.

Of course, she did. "Sure thing."

I get to my feet, straighten my tie, then slide my phone into my pocket. Something stirs in the pit of my stomach, sending a burst of energy rippling through my veins.

Lincoln and I might not be that different after all. We're both afraid of the women in our lives. Just for very, *very* different reasons.

Chapter Two

D ahlia

"A drink this weekend would be nice," I say, gazing across the manicured lawn outside my office window. "How about Friday after work?"

My best friend, Morgan, cheers through the phone.

"Stop it," I say, laughing. "It hasn't been that long. I just saw you two weeks ago."

"It feels like forever. Between my work trip and your relationship issues—"

"I don't have relationship issues anymore." I pivot on my heel. "I'm free to meet you for drinks—*ah!*" My hand claps against my chest. "*Damn you, Troy.*"

My heart skips a beat as I come to a screeching halt.

It's hard enough to stay calm when I have time to brace myself for Troy's presence. It's damn near impossible to appear unaffected when he blindsides me.

He sits across from my desk, relaxed in a chair, his knees spread.

A quick glance would give the impression that he's casually waiting for me to end my conversation. A deeper look says otherwise.

Troy Castelli's square jaw is tight. His gray eyes are nothing short of thunderstorm clouds just before lightning strikes. His elbow rests against the arm of the chair, and the pad of his thumb strokes his bottom lip as if he's deciding my fate.

He's a whole damn mood—a sexy, dangerous vibe that steals my breath.

"Pull yourself together," Morgan hisses through the phone. "I hear you panting from here."

I laugh, letting out a breath and standing taller. "I'm sorry about that, Morgan. A co-worker just *rudely* entered my office without knocking."

Troy lifts one brow and drops his hand. He couldn't look more bored if he tried.

"If you play your cards right, that won't be all he enters." She snickers.

"Drinks Friday, right?" I ask, ignoring her. "I'll call you later this week to pick a time and place."

"Yes, and don't try to bail on me. I need this."

I smile, holding Troy's gaze as I approach my desk. "I need it, too. Talk soon."

"Bye."

I end the call and place my phone next to my computer. Troy's eyes peer into mine as I get seated.

"Theo knocks," I say.

"As he should."

"As he should, huh?" I ask, leaning against my desk. "Then why shouldn't you?"

Troy only stares at me.

This man. "You're extra grumpy today. Want me to get you a snack?"

A wry little smile quirks his mouth.

I roll my eyes and awaken my computer. "I don't get paid enough to deal with you."

"Who was on the phone?"

I peer at him over my shoulder. "What?"

"Who was on the phone?" He sits up, holding my gaze hostage. "It didn't sound like a work conversation."

"What makes you say that?"

"You're meeting them for drinks on Friday—location to be determined. That sounds like a personal appointment to me."

I pull a *Troy* on him and lift a brow, giving him my best disinterested look. What he can't see are my insides melting into a pile of goo.

Troy and I have worked together since my first day at Landry Security. On paper, we shouldn't mesh well at all. He's moody and sullen. I wake up happy. He's pragmatic and sensible—infuriatingly so at times. I'm optimistic about most things, which irritates him to no end. Troy wants to keep everyone at arm's length, and I'm a hugger in every sense of the word. Despite all of that, we click.

Somehow.

"I wouldn't call it *an appointment*," I say, pulling my coffee mug toward me. I inhale a deep breath, hoping to fill my senses with the wonderful aroma of coffee. Instead, I get a lungful of Troy's cologne. It's seductive and masculine—promising excitement and a hint of danger.

It's fitting.

"What would *you* call it?" he asks.

The edge to his voice sends a chill down my spine. "I'd call it *none of your business*."

His eyes darken. I grin.

"I take it you saw Lincoln bright and early," I say before sipping my drink. "It's the only explanation for your uncontained joy this morning."

"You know, it still shocks me that he's Ford's brother."

"Right? Ford is Mr. Serious and Responsible, and Lincoln is ..."

"A dipshit."

I laugh. "I wasn't going to phrase it that way, but I mean, you aren't wrong."

Troy chuckles, too. "Nah, he's a good guy. I gotta be in the right mood for him, but he's easily managed. Just a headache."

"Ah, *look at you*," I tease. "You're getting soft on me, Castelli."

"There's nothing soft about me, Doll."

A flush stings my cheeks, just like it does each time he calls me *doll*. I know it's just a shortened version of my name. It's not a term of endearment. Still, it *feels* intimate, whether he means it to or not.

I shift in my seat. "Moving on, did you get your license renewed?"

"How could I ignore the three reminders on my calendar?"

"You couldn't. That's why they were there."

"I renewed it Saturday morning. I only had to wait in line for two hours." He grimaces. "Such a great way to spend my time."

"Why didn't you just do it online?"

"The system kept giving me an error."

"Poor you." I smile before taking another sip of my coffee. "Did Ford give you our next assignment?"

The corner of his mouth twitches. "*Our assignment*, huh?"

"Yes, *our assignment*. We're a team, remember?"

"How about you let me do the office part of our teamwork this time, and you can do the field work?"

I nod knowingly. "Finally."

"Finally what?"

"You're finally admitting that I'm badass."

He scoffs, shaking his head.

"You know it, Castelli. I mean, I'm not wearing a suit and tie, and I'm definitely wearing flat shoes because I can't chase bad guys in heels."

Amusement flickers in his eyes.

"But I'm observant, and I've been called scary a time or two," I say. "Heck, *you're* scared of me half the time."

"I love how you believe the shit you say."

"I love how you pretend you don't."

He watches me carefully with a hint of a smile. The lines on his face soften, and the tension in his shoulders eases.

A flood of warmth spreads throughout my body and pools in the apples of my cheeks. I take another drink, hoping the heat of the coffee will provide a solid excuse for the flush if he notices, and then reroute the conversation back to business.

"So what's next for us?" I ask.

He runs his hands down the arms of the chair and sighs. "I don't know. Ford gave me a choice."

"A choice? That's fun."

"Eh, not really."

"Want me to pick? I'm open-minded and levelheaded. I'd be good at this."

He stretches his long legs out in front of him.

"Let me guess," I say. "Option one is ... working with the Brewers again?"

"Nope."

"Okay. What about staying local with one of the Landrys?"

"Nope."

I lick my lips. "You've been clear that you don't want to return to the Laina Kelley contract. So I'm hoping it's not that."

The blaze of fire in his eyes tells me it's exactly that.

Irritation sweeps through me on Troy's behalf.

He has requested to be removed from the Kelley assignment more than once—and he doesn't make many requests or demands. Troy does whatever's asked of him, and he does a damn good job. The fact that Ford is asking Troy to return pisses me off.

"I hope you told him no," I say, my shoulders taut.

"Well, the other option isn't exactly stellar."

I set my mug down with a thud. "What was it?"

"He wants me to take a vacation." Troy sighs.

I bite my tongue both literally and figuratively.

Troy has taken one sick day since I started working here, and if HR can be believed, he's called in sick a total of three times while

15

employed by the Landry family. He gives his all to this company; his loyalty to Ford knows no bounds. And it really pisses me off that Ford, in turn, puts Troy in this position.

Even if I think he needs a vacation, too.

"What are you going to do?" I ask, my voice even.

"I don't fucking know. He told me he needs to know by Friday. So I guess I wait and hope another job comes up."

"Want me to tell Ford that I refuse to work on the Kelley case? If we both say we won't, what can he do?"

Troy's eyes twinkle. The moment of vulnerability makes my heart swell.

"I'll fight him." I grin. "I know Ford was like special ops or whatever, but he hasn't seen me with a baton. I was a majorette with the band in high school. I know how to work a stick."

"Is that so?"

"You can't possibly be surprised. I'm good at everything I do."

My stomach clenches at the heat in his eyes. Goose bumps run down my arms, and I struggle to change the subject. My brain fries with the imagery of me and a certain *stick*.

Thankfully, Troy does me a favor and changes it for me.

"So who are you having drinks with on Friday?" he asks, nibbling his bottom lip.

"I told you, it's none of your business."

"Is it Theo?"

"No." I laugh. "You really think I'd have drinks with Theo?"

He shrugs.

"Although *it's none of your business*," I repeat, "I'm going out with my friend Morgan. We haven't hung out in a while, so we're meeting up after work on Friday."

"The same Morgan who baked you the unicorn birthday cake?"

My lips part into a smile. "That's her. Good memory."

He shrugs again.

"She's been working out of town," I say. "And I've been dealing with my breakup from Freddy ..."

I know I've made a mistake as soon as I say Freddy's name.

Troy leans forward, resting his elbows on his knees. "What does that mean?"

"What does what mean?" I ask, knowing full well what he means.

"*Dealing with your breakup?*"

I groan. "It doesn't mean anything, Troy. It was a poor choice of words."

"You chose them."

"And now I un-choose them."

He rolls his head around his neck. "Cut the shit, Doll."

"You're my co-worker. I don't owe you an explanation."

He narrows his eyes. "No, you don't. But you're going to tell me anyway."

I fall back into my chair and cross my arms over my chest. Troy pins me to the seat with nothing but his gaze. The intensity makes me squirm.

The last thing I want to do is discuss Freddy—with anyone. But the last person in the world I want to talk about it with is Troy.

"We broke up," I say flatly. "Everything's fine. It's all good. Freddy's just having a hard time accepting reality, and it's been a bit of a process."

"Define that."

"I'd rather not."

His jaw flexes. "Is he fucking with you?"

"*No*," I say, sitting tall in a futile attempt at appearing in control. "I told you everything is fine. Now, let's stop talking about it. You were just on my ass for having a personal conversation at work, and now here you are prodding me into having a personal conversation with you."

"It's different."

"Hardly." I make a face at him. "Have you uploaded your paperwork from last week into the system? I need to get all your invoices coded and to accounting by noon."

He opens his mouth—I think to argue with me. To avoid that, I cut him off before he can say a word.

"I've scheduled your truck for maintenance tomorrow since you're in town," I say. "Take it to the shop in the morning. They'll have a loaner ready for you. And I'm going to schedule your physical for Wednesday. I was trying to figure out how to get you in to see Dr. Manning, but since you'll be here all week, I'll get him to squeeze you in. Cool?"

"I thought my physical was good through the end of the year?"

"You thought wrong. It expires in three weeks."

He smiles. It's a baby smile, but a smile nonetheless. "Let me know, and I'll be there."

"Good boy."

He groans, making me laugh.

"I have a lot of stuff to do today, so scram," I say, motioning toward the door. "Please upload your paperwork so I can process it this morning before Norm from accounting comes for me."

He pauses before gripping the armrests and getting to his feet.

His body unfolds from the chair inch by inch. Each movement sends a drift of his cologne my way. I look up at his six-foot-three-inch frame, broad shoulders, and barrel chest as he peers down at me. It's hard not to shiver.

"Thanks," he says with a small nod.

"For what?"

He shrugs, letting his gaze linger on me before turning to the door. "Last week's paperwork will be in the system within the hour."

"Thank you."

He pulls open the door and looks over his shoulder. "One more thing."

"What's that?"

"Tell Freddy to accept reality, or I'll help him."

My jaw drops as Troy tucks his chin to his chest and slips out of my office. He pulls the door shut behind him.

I inhale a long, deep, steadying breath and blow it out.

If Troy were anyone else, and I met him anywhere else, I would give in to this attraction in a heartbeat. I'd be putty in that man's sexy, calloused hands. But as luck will have it, instead of whispering how much he wants to fuck me, he just fucks with me.

Why does he have to be so complicated?

I grin.

Why does he have to be so damn gorgeous?

My grin slides into a pout.

And why do I have to be so damn attracted to the one man who's absolutely off-limits?

I sigh and get back to work.

Chapter Three

Dahlia

"Home, sweet home," I say, pressing the fob until my car horn beeps three times behind me.

A soft breeze blows gently across the driveway, bringing the sweet scent of flower blossoms with it. Blazing oranges, vivid reds, and majestic purples paint the early evening sky. Children laugh in the distance.

Rows of tidy homes, their windows reflecting the warm glow of the setting sun, line the neighborhood's charming streets. Ferns hang from porches. Bikes lay unattended on front lawns. Nearly every address has a barbecue, something I found amusing when I moved in a year ago.

Now, I have one, too.

"There's my girlfriend," a voice calls from my left. I glance over my shoulder to see my neighbor Burt waving his wrinkled hand from his porch swing.

I laugh. "Hey there, handsome. How was your day?"

"It's better now that you're home. Need some help? You look like you're about to drop all that stuff."

Three takeout boxes fill my hands, and my gym bag dangles from the crook of my left arm.

"I don't need help carrying anything," I say. "But I do happen to have an extra hamburger from Hillary's House if you're hungry."

His eyes light up so brightly that I can see them from my porch.

I open the front door, leaving it that way so Burt can enter behind me. I drop my bag onto a chair and carry the food containers to the kitchen. Last night's stir-fry hangs in the air as I deposit tonight's dinner on the counter.

The kitchen's what sold me on this townhouse. A skylight allows so much sunshine into the space that it just *feels* happy. Whoever designed the room wasted no space, adding as much storage as possible. The refrigerator is also brand-new and *almost* too big for the space—which I love. It houses my collection of magnets dating back to my childhood.

I shake my head and grin, returning my newest additions to their spot in the top right corner. Morgan gave them to me as a joke for my birthday two weeks ago following a conversation about sex. They're both circles with a water gun in the center, and the words *I squirt* are printed around the edge of one magnet, and *Super Soaker* is printed around the other.

Burt immediately noticed them and teased me about stories he could share if I wanted to hear them. I didn't. Now he screws with me by moving them around my refrigerator from time to time.

"Hamburgers from Hillary's House, huh?" Burt asks.

"And chocolate cake."

"That's pretty fancy for a Monday night."

I smile at him. "We're celebrating."

"I'm all for a good celebration, but it helps to know the occasion. Should I have picked you some of the neighbor's flowers? I could've blamed it on those boys across the street. The oldest one walked their dog this morning, and the little fucker shit in my yard."

My giggle isn't appreciated. "Did you make him clean it up?"

He waves a hand through the air. "Nah, I did it after he went home."

My giggle turns into a laugh.

"But I am gonna tell him next time to bring a poop bag, or else I'm going to throw it in their yard," he says, fighting a smile. "Now, what are we celebrating?"

"You're looking at a girl who was able to run not four but *five* miles today after work. I thought that deserved a treat."

"Doesn't a burger and cake defeat the purpose of running five miles?"

"Absolutely not."

His bushy brows tug together. "If you think about it, running five miles was a treat to your health. You don't need a coffee or cake treat, too."

"Sounds like *you* need a treat," I say, winking at him.

He rolls his eyes.

"Besides," I say, grabbing water for me and a sugar-free soda I keep just for Burt from the fridge, "you're being awfully judgy for someone who's going to partake in said treat."

We sit at the small table near the window overlooking my backyard. Burt digs into his dinner before I get situated. I can't help but wonder if he had lunch.

Burt and I have been *best neighbors*, as he calls us, since the day I moved in. It was his seventy-fifth birthday, and he spent it, much to their dismay, supervising the college kids unloading my boxes from a big truck. He raced across our adjoining lawns when they nearly broke my headboard and kept an eye on them. I introduced myself, he did the same, and we've been a dynamic duo ever since.

"Heard from Freddy?" Burt asks, wiping his mouth with a napkin.

My stomach tightens. "Yes, actually. He texted me today. A few times."

"What's he texting you for?"

"He thinks I have a pair of his sunglasses, but I don't."

"Does he really think that, or is he just trying to get your attention? Or is he trying to come over here to bother you?"

I smile at the concern in Burt's big brown eyes. "Who knows?" I stand and head to my bag to retrieve my phone. "If I were a betting woman, I'd say he pawned them."

"Yeah, you're probably right. I'm glad you woke up and got rid of that boy."

While I read Freddy's last text, Burt continues his monologue, detailing all the reasons Freddy was a bad boyfriend.

Freddy: Just let me come by and look. I know where I would've left them. Besides, you don't need to waste your time looking for them, baby. I know how busy you are.

"Dating you was a waste of my time," I mutter, returning to the table.

Me: They aren't here.

He wastes no time in responding.

Freddy: I just want to see you.

I groan, turning my phone face down next to my food.

"You texted him back, didn't you?" Burt asks.

"Yes. In my optimistic brain, I could tell him the glasses weren't here, and he'd go away—at least for a while. But he moved right into *I*

23

just want to see you," I say, mocking his tone. "It's been six weeks. When will he get the picture that we're done forever?"

"Probably never. Face it—you're a catch. Any young man with half a brain inside his head would want to date you. Hell, they should want to marry you, but you kids these days aren't into marriage like we were back in my time."

I nibble on the end of a fry. "I want to be married someday."

"That doesn't surprise me."

It surprises me. I pop the rest of the fry into my mouth.

As I grew up, marriage was never an aspiration. I saw my single mother navigate her life without a man. She worked two jobs, raised me, and seemed content. All I wanted in life was to be her—independent, strong, and happy.

It was only after her death that I began to understand the truth.

And now, armed with this information, I crave the happily ever after Mom didn't get. I don't want to grow old alone. I don't want to fall asleep by myself every night. I want to know what it's like to be loved by someone fully and completely.

I also want to love someone back.

"What kind of man could you see yourself marrying?" Burt asks. "I'm guessing I'm too old."

I laugh. "Well, I do hope to have kids, and I think you had a vasectomy, so ..."

He laughs, too, lines crinkling around his eyes. "Yeah. That's the problem—my vasectomy."

"Can't blame that on me."

"Can't blame that on me, either. When you're an over-the-road trucker and want to be sure you don't knock someone up in your travels, you do what you gotta do."

We chuckle softly.

"I don't know what kind of man I'd like to marry," I say, lifting another fry. "He'd have to be smart. Funny. Someone who could be strong enough to protect his family but gentle enough to hold a baby."

Burt grins.

My brain immediately envisions Troy with a baby, and I try not to swoon at the table. That would be too hot to be safe. I don't think I'd survive that reality.

"He'd probably be six-three or so," I say, picturing Troy standing in the doorway to my office. "Dark hair cut close to his head. Gray eyes. Heavy brows. He'd look just as good in an expensive suit as he does in sweats and a T-shirt."

"Sounds mighty specific."

"I'm building an imaginary boyfriend. I might as well get what I want, right?"

"Might as well." He nods toward my food. "Eat up. I'll get forks, and we can dig into that cake."

I nod as he leaves for the kitchen. "Don't bother my magnets."

"Wouldn't dream of it."

I breathe and try to settle the thudding of my heart.

Troy's smirk blazes through my mind, sending heat waves pulsing through me.

Our exchange this morning left me thrown off all day. I kept thinking I heard his voice in the office. I smelled his cologne down the halls. Every ping of an email or text message had me racing to see if it was him.

It was ridiculous.

It was the reason I ran five freaking miles. I needed to work that shit out of my body and clear my head.

Troy Castelli is my co-worker. Period. End of. He may be the object of my dreams, but he has to stay in my dreams. That's unfortunate and unreasonable, but it's also the way things are.

"Here's a fork," Burt says, handing me the utensil. "Do I have to wait on you, or can I go ahead and celebrate now?"

I push the cake to him. "Celebrate away."

"I saw your daddy on the news today," Burt says, taking a slice and putting it in the top of his takeout container.

"Fantastic."

"For the record, I think it's all a bunch of bullshit. Unpopular opinion, I know."

"You could say that. But I do appreciate you giving him the benefit of the doubt."

He shoves a forkful of cake into his mouth, watching me warily.

A lump settles at the base of my throat. I stand, ignoring another incoming text, and gaze out the window.

Being the daughter of Joseph Dallo still takes some getting used to. The mere fact of having a father for the last year and a half after not having one for twenty-four years was jarring in and of itself. But it's more complicated than that. He's also a conundrum.

To me, he's been nothing but kind, considerate, and thoughtful. I've found him to be wildly intelligent, well-mannered, and respectful. But, to the rest of the world, he's everything but those things. That can be very confusing.

"I talked to him last night." I cross my arms protectively over my midsection. "He said he had court this morning but was upbeat about it. He seemed certain things would go his way."

"This isn't his first rodeo with the law, sweet pea. He knows what he's doing. And he has a hell of a good troop of attorneys around him. He's in good hands."

I hum, not convinced by Burt's words. But what do I know? It *is* my first rodeo.

"Do you know what bothers me the most about this whole thing?" I ask, facing Burt again.

His forehead wrinkles, but he says nothing.

"I hate that you're the only one who gives him the benefit of the doubt." I take my seat again. "It's probably because I've only known him for a year and a half, and I'm not exactly well versed in the recycling business or really understand money laundering. But I believe him when he says he's innocent."

My cheeks burn with embarrassment. I'm foolish to admit that out loud because I've read the reports in the papers and online. The case against my father for laundering money for the Magne, a rising cartel based in the Upper Midwest, is strong. He looks as guilty as sin. Logic says he's guilty, too. Maybe it's because I don't want to think I'm the child of a man that dirty, but when he tells me he's innocent, I don't think he's lying. Even if I hate admitting that because I know I sound naive. And even though I know liars are really good at pretending they're not one.

"Then you believe him," Burt says. "But please be safe. Regardless of whether he's guilty or not, the man has connections. He has business dealings. His industry isn't filled with nuns and holy water, you know?"

I give him a half grin.

Burt sighs, laying his fork on the edge of his plate. "You didn't eat your celebration cake."

"I know. I'll eat it after my shower. I have five miles of sweat on me, and I'm beginning to stink."

I glance down at my phone.

> Freddy: Dammit, Dahlia. I just want to talk to you. I need you, baby. I can't live without you. You know that. You're my entire world.

Right.

"Promise?" Burt asks.

"Promise."

We clean up quietly. Burt carefully places my cake in the refrigerator and throws away our garbage. I wipe down the table.

"Thanks for dinner, sweet pea," Burt says. "Can I do anything for you?"

"I'm good. Your presence was all I needed."

He chuckles, tossing up a wave, and lets himself out.

I pick my phone up off the table, intending to shove it in my pocket on my way upstairs. But as I turn to the staircase, I stop and glance at the screen.

A slow smile stretches across my lips.

> Troy: I just got a confirmation text from Dr. Manning's office.

I bang out my response.

> Me: I'm glad that worked out. <smiling emoji>

> Troy: Settle down.

> Me: <confused emoji>

> Troy: You abuse emoji.

I snort. Whatever.

> Me: How else will you know what my face is doing? Texts are so easily misconstrued. I like my messages to feel personal and clear.

> Troy: Trust me. I know what your face is doing.

> Me: Well, I can't trust you because I can't read your face. You could be typing that angrily or cheekily or flatly or conversationally. How am I supposed to know?

> Troy: What did people do before emoji?

Me: Lived very boring, muted lives.

Troy: Yet they survived.

I laugh.

Me: There will come a day, Mr. Castelli, when you use an emoji.

Troy: Unlikely. What time does my truck go into the shop tomorrow?

I lean against the wall, smiling as I type.

Me: By nine. That's on your calendar, you know.

Troy: Yes. It's on my calendar for midnight. My assistant's getting rusty.

Me: <gasps> Your assistant's probably just overworked.

Troy: My assistant's many things. Overworked is not one of them.

Me: I beg to differ. But you're right when you say I'm many things. I'm basically a Renaissance woman.

Troy: Have you been drinking?

Me: Not yet. Have you?

Troy: It's Monday.

Me: And your point ... <confused emoji>

Troy: I'll see you tomorrow.

"I'll be looking forward to it, Mr. Castelli."

Me: Can't tell if that's a threat or a promise.

Troy: That will give you something to ponder.

Me: See you tomorrow. Good night. <moon emoji>

Troy: Good night.

I smile all the way up the stairs.

Chapter Four

Troy

"She specifically requests you."

I growl, slipping off my jacket and tossing it over the back of a chair in the foyer. My conversation with Ford earlier echoes through my brain as I walk down the hallway.

"If I do that, you're taking option two."

"Fuck," I mumble, removing my shirt and tie, and throwing them like a football into the laundry room as I pass. They fall unceremoniously into the center of the basket next to the washer.

The evening sun drenches the house in a muted glow. The warmth that bathes the white walls reminds me of a picture from a magazine. A rainbow stretches across the black leather sofa as if a pot of gold sits on the other side, not a gray rug.

The golden hour is my favorite time of the day. Everything is a bit warmer, a little softer—a striking difference from my normal course of business. Moments like this, when I'm tucked away in my home and surrounded by my favorite things, are what I most look forward to when the sun is shining.

And that's becoming a problem.

I let out a breath and allow my shoulders to fall.

"Want me to tell Ford that I refuse to work on the Kelley case? If we both say we won't, what can he do?"

I smile at the memory—and from the warmth rippling throughout my body, a product of Dahlia's response.

Her reply came immediately. *Fiercely.* She unequivocally had my back.

It's so fucking sexy. *She's so fucking sexy.*

She's a standalone in a trio of people who I absolutely trust, something I struggle with daily. Ford and I have been through some serious shit, and he's never wavered. He's always had my back. And my brother, Travis, has been my ride or die since the day he was born. We, too, have battled through unsavory situations and came out on the other side as survivors because we had each other. But Dahlia? There's no reason for her to be so loyal to me. Yet I don't question it—although I probably should.

"What the fuck am I going to do?" I groan, pulling my phone from my pocket. I set aside my thoughts and answer my brother's call.

"Hey, Trav," I say, entering the kitchen.

"Hey. Are you home by any chance? I had to run to the hardware store five minutes from your house. Thought I'd stop by if you aren't busy."

"I'm here. About to make a sandwich. Want one?"

"I'll do you one better. I'm in the drive-through right now. Want a burger?"

"Sure."

"Be there in a minute."

The call ends, and I slide my phone onto the countertop. I grab a bottle of water and head to the living room.

Guilt weighs heavy on my shoulders as I sink into my favorite chair near the fireplace. Ford's offer lingers in my head, reminding me of the decision that must be made. It's a choice that most people would kill for, and I'm a fuck for being put out by it.

Do I take a fantastic job that pays entirely too much or a paid vacation that pays more than I deserve? *What terrible options.*

I sigh, resting my head against the chair and closing my eyes. The stillness of the house covers me, helping me recenter. As the tension I've carried all day eases across the back of my neck, the truth finds an opening to slip into focus.

It's not the job or the vacation that has me frustrated. It's not Laina's screaming fanbase or having too much time on my hands.

It's my life.

"Knock, knock," Travis says as the front door opens and then closes. "They were out of pickles. Can you believe that shit? How does a fast-food joint run out of pickles?" He drops a bag onto my lap. "That would be like you running out of bullshit. It's a main ingredient of the brand."

"Did you work on that analogy all the way over here?"

"No, it just came to me in the moment. I'm brilliant like that."

We exchange a smile.

My younger brother tears into his meal with the same gusto he's had since he was a toddler. The nostalgia warms my heart. The reason behind it cools it just as fast.

"Slow down," I tell him, taking my burger from the bag like a civilized individual. "You're gonna make yourself sick."

"I know." He chuckles around a mouthful of french fries. "I forget that I'm a grown-ass man who has his own money and can buy all the food he wants."

He swallows so much at once that I can see it move down his throat.

"So what did you do today?" I ask.

"I about fell off a roof."

"You like to keep things interesting, don't you?"

He grins. "Says the guy who intentionally puts himself in the line of fire daily."

I unwrap my burger, remove the onions, and take a bite.

"As I was hanging off the gutter, waiting on Bradley to bring me a ladder, I had a moment to ponder life and its great mysteries."

"Oh really?" I ask, amused. It's hard to tell if Travis is serious and almost fell or if he's making up a story to entertain me. He developed the skill over the many days we would walk the neighborhood, waiting to be let back into the house. We were two kids with no business wandering the streets and seeing and hearing things we had no business witnessing. "What did you come up with?"

"More questions than answers, really. For example, if you consume half of a five-hour energy drink, do you get two and a half hours of energy, or five hours' worth in two and a half hours?"

I chuckle, shaking my head.

"When you're at the movie theater, which armrest is yours? It can't be both because every other person won't have one. I mean, the newer theaters have individual seats, so the obvious answer is to go to one of them. But the older ones are more cost-effective for a guy on a budget, so it's a problem. Also, why is there a caloric number on a pack of gum? You're chewing it, not eating it."

"And you thought of all this while hanging on the gutter?"

"Yeah. Then I realized the number nine is brown, and that really fucked me up."

Huh? "You know what? I'm not even going to touch that one."

He shrugs, unbothered, and shoves half of his burger into his mouth. He speaks again, but it's garbled.

"It's perfectly acceptable to wait until you swallow to talk," I say.

Travis rolls his eyes, swallows, and then reaches for his drink. "I asked you what you did today."

"I'm in the office this week, so I got caught up on paperwork. Ford had me ride along to a couple of meetings this afternoon. Otherwise, not much."

"Where are you heading next?"

I put my burger on the wrapper and exhale. Travis slows his chewing and sets his down as well. He understands what I'm about to say without me saying it—the gist of it anyway. The ability to read each other like a book is the product of our youth.

"What's going on?" he asks, his brow lifted.

The tension I've been warring with since this morning pulls at the back of my neck again. I run a hand over the top of my head and scratch my scalp. The pain causes my nervous system to release endorphins, which helps my irritation. That's helpful because I won't take my mood out on my brother.

"If I tell you, you'll laugh," I say.

"Try me."

One corner of my mouth tugs toward the ceiling. "I have to decide whether to return to Laina's team or to take a vacation."

"If it were me," he says, popping a single fry into his mouth, "I'd take the vacation."

"I knew you'd say that."

Travis sighs and rests his elbows on his knees. "Look, we deal with our childhood trauma differently. You keep yourself in amped-up situations so you can't think about all the shit our parents did to us. I take the opposite approach and joke about everything to avoid my emotions."

"Your point?"

"My point is that my way of coping is better. At least I have fun."

I roll my eyes.

"I'm serious," he says, laughing. "You have to balance things out—trade bullets for beaches. Shots for sand. Clients for—"

"Enough." I shake my head, chuckling. "That's enough analogies for one day."

"What would be so terrible about getting away for a while?"

"It's not that," I admit, putting my food next to Travis's on the coffee table and then standing. "I mean, that's a part of it. A big part of it. But it's just ..."

I wander around my living room, taking in the decor on the walls and mantel—a collection of images and memorabilia hand-picked to make me not want to jump out of the window.

The guys from my unit and me in front of a truck moments after one of them learned he'd just become a father. A statue I bought in Italy on a whim. A picture of Travis and me on his twenty-first birthday—just before he puked all over my shirt. There's a snapshot of our dog, Ralph, sitting beside me and Travis that I included because the way our faces are lit up in laughter is one of the few childhood images I have that capture a genuine happiness from that period.

I just have to forget that Dad kicked Ralph so hard a few minutes after Mom took this picture that Ralph limped for the rest of his life.

My eyes close, and I shove the memory out of my mind.

My life has been lived, and it's been lived a hell of a lot harder and faster than most people. I've traveled, survived explosions, and saved lives. I've partied, read books, and climbed a volcano. I have a job I love, a house I never imagined I would afford, and a small number of people around me who I care about deeply. But still ...

"It's just what?" Travis asks.

I lean against the fireplace and look at my brother. "I don't know. Pointless, maybe. Hollow. What's the purpose of it all?"

His face sobers.

"I'm being dramatic." I stop. "You know, I *was* around Lincoln Landry all day. It kind of makes sense that I'm acting like an asshole."

Travis laughs.

I move back to my chair and sit. "You're right when you say I've chosen to live a life that keeps me occupied, and I've loved every damn minute of it. It's afforded me a great standard of living."

"Speaking of which, will you pay me back for dinner?"

I ignore him. "But the danger I used to get off on isn't thrilling anymore. The high-pressure shit isn't as exciting."

"So *take a vacation.*"

"And then what? Sit around, thinking about all of the shit that's gone wrong in my life?"

"I hear it's good to face your demons."

"Then why don't you do it?"

"I've been fucking Lola. I've done more than face a demon lately. A demon would be a walk in the park."

I grin.

"Maybe you need someone to spend time with. Have you seen anyone in a while?"

"This isn't a problem I can fuck my way out of, Trav, but thanks."

"It couldn't hurt to try."

Instead of answering him, I flip on the television.

"Leave it to you to watch the local evening news," Travis says. "I didn't know that was still a thing."

I motion for him to pay attention to the headlines and not me.

"Have you seen anyone in a while?"

Travis's question wasn't meant to be serious ... I don't think. Little does he know that's the crux of my problem.

I'm fucking lonely.

A burning sensation prickles my chest.

It hit me a few weeks ago in the middle of the night. I woke up at three in the morning after a nightmare and, for the first time in my life, wished that someone was here. That I wasn't alone. That the bed beside me wasn't empty. That someone might be here when I came home from work, excited to see me.

The idea has followed me ever since. Eating alone has bothered me. Sitting in the living room and reading a book by myself feels off. Everything I've done, everything I've enjoyed up until the nightmare, all feels ... wrong. Less. Incomplete.

But what can I do?

Maybe it's a midlife crisis. I did turn thirty-seven last month. It's the only explanation for why the job I love no longer fulfills me. It must be why I'm suddenly wishing, or at least considering, that I had a significant other—something I've intentionally avoided most of my life. There's no other reason I'm suddenly wishing I could have more in my life when I know I can't. People don't change directions that fast without a catalyst.

"Hey, isn't that Dahlia's dad?" Travis asks, pointing at the screen.

I turn up the volume.

"In other news, Joseph Dallo was in court this morning. As you'll recall, Dallo, owner of the scrap metal recovery and recycling company known as Dallo Metalworks, is accused of money laundering, mail and wire fraud, and drug conspiracy by prosecutors. George Lee is at the courthouse with the latest. George, can you tell us what happened today?"

A man in a red shirt fills the screen. "Hi, Simone. Attorneys were in court this morning to discuss the defense's motion to suppress evidence. The defense claims Dallo's constitutional rights were violated, and all related evidence is thereby inadmissible. The judge is expected to rule on the motion next week. We'll keep you posted. Back to you, Simone."

I turn the volume down and toss the remote next to my burger.

My stomach tightens as I think about Dahlia.

"That trial's going to be a shit show," Travis says.

"No doubt."

"Has Dahlia said anything about it?"

I scrub my hand down my face. "No, not really. I get the impression she doesn't want to discuss it, so I don't bring it up. It's none of my business, anyway."

Travis looks at me, unimpressed.

"We'd only been working together for about six months when she found out Dallo was her father," I say. "We talked about him a little then. She brought it up when he was arrested, but that's about it."

"It would have to be hard for her to know that everyone knows her dad is accused of working with a cartel."

I lift a brow. He lifts his right back.

"Yeah, well, we know a thing or two about that," I mutter, sitting back again.

"No one really knows she's Dallo's daughter, though, right? Isn't that what you said?"

I nod. "Yeah. When the whole thing happened and Dallo contacted her, Dahlia was in disbelief for a while. All she knew about him was that he was shady. They agreed to keep her identity quiet and not make it public information. Seems like a good call, in retrospect."

"Dammit." Travis glances at his phone. "I'm sorry, Troy. I gotta get going. I need to drop a load of tools off at the jobsite before they lock it up for the night, and Bradley just texted me that they're winding down over there." He gets to his feet and reaches for his trash.

"I'll clean up. Don't worry about it."

He grins. "Thanks. Hit me up if you're not busy this weekend, and we'll hang out."

"Will do."

"Later."

"Bye."

He leaves, the door closing swiftly behind him.

I blow out a breath and sink into the leather.

"... *money laundering, mail and wire fraud, and drug conspiracy by prosecutors.*"

My throat burns as I imagine Dahlia listening to that. She's so tough, so sweet—so undeserving of being tied up in that shit. But you'd never know it. She always has a smile on her pretty face.

I nibble at my bottom lip, wondering if there's anything I can do for her. *Is she okay? Should I ask her about it or leave it alone?* I have no damn clue.

Even if the world doesn't know Dallo is her father, she does.

And I do.

And it fucking bothers me.

My jaw flexes as I consider all the ways that relationship could hurt her.

And all the ways I'd destroy the person responsible.

Chapter Five

Dahlia

"This is not great for my hair." I adjust my sunglasses and hit the gas. "But screw it. YOLO, baby."

The wind blows through my window and out the other side of the car, using the cab as a makeshift tunnel. The dice hanging off my rearview mirror dance in the breeze as dust particles twinkle around me.

The morning is bright. Traffic is light. My coffee is strong. And it's Tuesday, so I could sleep in an extra two hours because Ford Landry is kind like that. We get five personal hours a week to do with what we see fit—and we get paid for them. I use two on Tuesdays for sleep.

I crank up the radio's volume and perform the best concert my commuter buddies in the cars around me have ever seen. Tone on pitch ... ish. Hair in proper nineties wildness and more passion than the song probably warrants. But just before we're to the part where I get to rap about waterfalls, my phone rings through the speakers.

"Every time," I mutter, returning the volume to a respectable level. I answer the call as the windows slide back to their starting position. "Hello?"

"Dahlia?"

I smile at the warmth in his tone. "Why do you sound surprised? Didn't *you* call *me?*"

"You sound out of breath," Troy says.

"I just got done running ten miles. Set my new personal record."

He pauses. "Seriously?"

"Hell, no." I laugh. "But I was performing an excellent rendition of a nineties classic on my way to the office. Why? What's up?"

"I've been texting you for the last ten minutes."

I pull my sunglasses on top of my head. "First of all, I'm under no obligation to text you back within a ten-minute or sixty-minute or whatever-minute span. Second of all, George Strait was the first act of today's concert, and you don't interrupt the king, sir. Not for anyone."

He mumbles something I can't hear. That's probably for the best.

"Do you actually need something?" I ask. "Or did you text me a sweet *good morning,* and I didn't respond, so you got butt hurt?"

"*Right.*" I can practically hear him rolling his eyes. "I'm sitting at the shop. They're telling me it will be this afternoon when they finish, and they don't have any loaner cars available."

"Sucks to be you."

"*Doll.*"

I shift in my seat, happy he can't see the way I swoon. "*Troy.*"

"Fine. I'll call Becca and have her pick me up."

"*You will do no such thing,*" I say before I can catch myself. I clear my throat. "She's busy today."

"How busy can she possibly be? Theo is in a meeting with Ford. I'm sure she can spare a few minutes to help me out."

"I'll be there in ten."

"If you insist."

The amusement in his tone—wonderfully thick and rich—would

41

be foreplay if it wasn't at my expense. But it's my fault. I played right into his hands and handed him a victory.

I click the button on my steering wheel and end the call.

"I wasn't prepared for this," I say, groaning as I hit the brake at a red light. My vanity mirror is clean, *thank God*, and I use it to pull my hair into a messy bun.

It takes three lights until I'm properly powdered, lipstick'd, and put together. I'm straightening my shirt when I roll up to the curb outside the auto shop. Light bounces off the glass door as it opens.

Oh fuck.

My mouth hangs wide open.

If he didn't wake up this morning, look in the mirror, and wonder how he should dress to drive me absolutely out of my freaking mind, I'd be shocked.

Dark denim hugs his thick thighs. A tight black shirt skims his barrel chest, and a blazer hangs open in the front. He moves gracefully—confidently—with so much swagger that a man and a woman stop independently and stare.

Pull yourself together, Dahlia.

He reaches for the door when my phone rings through the car. I jump, hitting the button to answer it accidentally.

Troy climbs in, looking at me over the rim of his sunglasses before removing them altogether.

The slate gray of his eyes and the spicy, almost tobacco-y scent of his cologne team up to ruin me.

"Dahlia? Are you there?" a voice rings from my speakers.

Troy's brows pull together.

Focus. "Yes. Sorry. Hi. Who is this?"

"Hey. It's Theo."

Troy sits back and latches his seat belt. His lips press into a tight line.

"Hey, Theo," I say with a touch too much cheer and pull away from the curb. "What's going on?"

"I just got out of a meeting with Ford. It looks like I'll be working from the office for the next six weeks."

Troy bristles at my side.

"Oh really?" I ask, smiling. I like Theo and all, but I really couldn't care less where he works. What I do care about, and thoroughly enjoy, is Troy's annoyance with this piece of information. *I win this one, buddy.* "Why?"

"Our contract ran out in New York and they didn't renew. Ford asked if I wanted to work with Lincoln and his family when they move to Tennessee. Apparently, Lincoln is set to manage the Arrows baseball team."

"Cool! Maybe he can get us tickets."

"That's what I said." Theo laughs. "But they don't leave for a couple of months, and there isn't a short contract for me in the meantime."

Troy mumbles something under his breath that I can't make out.

"Sign up for snacks with Becca," I say, hitting my turn signal and pulling onto the main road leading to the office.

"Snacks?" He laughs. "What for?"

"Um, the office. We're snack-y. You have to pull your own weight around there."

"What is this? Kindergarten?"

I laugh, too. "I'll have you know that when we implemented a snack protocol in the office, our efficiency increased tenfold."

"How does it work?"

"Every Wednesday, someone brings in a snack. There's a sign-up form and list of allergies in Becca's office. Here's a tip. Only bring in homemade stuff if you can actually cook or bake. If not, prepackaged works just fine."

"Sounds like you had a bad experience at some point," he says.

"More than one."

Troy sits up, his arm brushing against mine. "Hey, Theo, something came up. She'll have to discuss snacks with you later."

"What?" he asks just before Troy ends the call on my dash.

43

"*Hey*," I say, looking at him over my shoulder. "What the heck was that?"

He stares straight ahead.

"That was rude, Troy."

"Oh, give me a break," he says. "He was wasting your time."

I snort. "No, he wasn't. We were having a friendly chat about work. And, even if he was wasting my time, it would be just that. *My time.*"

"You aren't that dense, Dahlia."

"Excuse me?"

"He was flirting with you."

"*He wasn't flirting with me.*"

Troy's head tilts to the side, nonplussed.

"Whatever," I say, sitting taller. *Troy cares that Theo was flirting with me? Huh.* "It was still rude."

"Well then, please forgive me."

I shake my head. "If you could say it like you meant it even a little, I might."

He shrugs, clearly unbothered.

"You know, I was having a damn good day until you got in my car," I say, slowing as a light changes to yellow.

"I was having a pretty decent day until I got in here, too."

I look at him, fully intending to glare. But when our eyes connect, my intentions fall to the wayside. Our gazes lock, and an entire conversation takes place within a handful of seconds—and neither of us utters a word.

My stomach flutters as my body heat rises. I suck in a hasty breath, fighting not to lose myself in his eyes.

"You can go," he says, his words soft.

A horn blares at me from behind, waking me from my momentary haze.

I face the road and hit the gas, exhaling slowly.

"Sorry for ruining your day." He's probably fighting a grin, but I refuse to look. "I mean the apology this time."

"I'll accept it then."

Out of my peripheral vision, I catch his fingers flexing against his jeans.

"What do you have going on today?" I ask.

"Working on a security plan for a gala Ford's parents are throwing in a few months. They have the same party every year. So it's more about updating protocol than starting from scratch." He flexes his fingers again. "And I need to talk to him about a few things."

"Did you decide what you're doing next?"

"Nope."

I hum. "I'm still leaning toward vacation."

"You and Travis. He tried to talk me into it last night."

"I knew I liked your brother."

"I do, too. Most of the time."

We exchange a quick grin.

"He came over last night," Troy says, hesitating. "Asked about you, actually."

"Why?"

He takes a long, deep breath. "We watched the news, and they did a piece on your father."

Oh. My shoulders stiffen. "I see. That wasn't where I thought you were going with that, but okay."

"Where'd you think I was going with it?"

I don't know where I thought he was going, but the turn to my father's legal issues gave me whiplash.

"Doll, if you don't want to talk about this, we won't."

"It's ... fine," I say, forcing a swallow down my throat. "It's just awkward going from not having a father at all to having one. And then not being able to talk about him openly. Then with the few people you can talk to about it, things like money laundering and fraud come up. Kinda hard to make those adjustments on the fly, you know?"

Troy shifts in his seat. "I don't give a fuck about your father, to be honest. I only wondered how *you* were doing."

45

His genuine concern slays me. It hits me smack dab in the middle of my heart.

"It's too much to process in one car ride, that's for sure," I say, widening my eyes to keep tears from spilling down my cheeks.

We sit quietly while I drive through the beautiful streets of Savannah. Troy doesn't push me to talk, and I'm grateful for that—just like I'm grateful he asked. It's such a weird position to be in. On the one hand, knowing someone sees you and cares about you is wonderful. On the other hand, being seen pricks a person's vulnerability. And if there's one thing that makes me antsy these days, it's being vulnerable.

I turn onto the road leading to Landry Security when a text cuts through the air. Freddy's name is printed across my dash for everyone, *for Troy*, to see.

"You're popular today," he says, unamused.

I swiftly swipe the notification away.

Another one pops up.

Troy stares holes into the side of my face.

I swipe Freddy's second and third texts off the screen. "He thinks he left his sunglasses at my house."

"That's not true, and you know it."

I sigh. "Yeah. I know it."

We pull into the parking lot, and I back the car into my spot. The engine stops, but we don't move. We sit together in the comfortable silence.

The safety of the space—of the car, parked next to Ford, and sitting next to Troy—allows me to let my guard down and breathe.

Troy didn't have to ask how I was doing, but he did. He could've talked shop or sat in silence, but he chose to inquire on a personal level. That matters to me. There's a sweetness under those heavy brows and that mass of muscle. I wish I could see it more.

"Thank you," I say.

"For what?"

I shrug, looking straight ahead at the block building. "I don't want to say *you care* because God knows you'd have an aneurysm if anyone labeled you as having emotions." I glance at him and grin. "But despite your rudeness to my friends ..."

His eyes narrow, making me laugh.

"And your assumption that I'm going to text you right back ... and the way you intentionally irritate the hell out of me, you carefully go beyond being my co-worker in a way that means a lot to me." I lean toward him, then regret that move immediately. He smells divine. *Why can't he be an overbearing, decrepit, stinks-to-high-heaven ogre?* "You aren't creepy. That's what that means."

"Good to know."

"Now, you're going to buy me lunch today, or I'm going to tell everyone in the office you're nice."

He groans and opens his door.

"I want a good lunch, too," I say, climbing out of the car. "There's that little deli two streets over with the monster chocolate chip cookies that they serve warm. Do you know the one I mean?"

He holds the door to the building open for me. "I thought you wanted lunch?"

"I do."

"Then why are we talking about cookies?"

I hit the fob and my car horn goes off once, twice, and then three times. Troy shakes his head, muttering something about overkill, and follows me inside.

"Because cookies are dessert," I say. "And dessert is the biggest part of lunch. You can have a little before the meal as a reward for making it halfway through the day. Then you eat for sustenance. Then you finish it with another piece of dessert to get you through the rest of your day."

"You don't need a reward for everything in life, you know."

"Why do people keep saying that to me?"

He stops at my office door and faces me. Flecks of gold sparkle in his eyes. "Do you want ham and provolone, lettuce, tomatoes, and pickle? Honey mustard and light mayo?"

My smile splits my cheeks. "And two cookies."

"Of course." He heads down the hallway. "And two cookies."

I laugh and get to work with the promise of lunch as a motivator.

Who am I trying to kid?

Seeing Troy again is the real dessert ... and, *thank God*, he doesn't even know it.

Chapter Six

Dahlia

"That class just kicked my ass," I say, smiling at the owner of the yoga studio I've frequented for a couple of years. "Where do you find these instructors?"

Mallory laughs. "You should see the ones I *don't* hire. I'm doing you a favor."

"That's ... scary." I laugh, too. "I'll see you on Friday."

"See you then."

I give her a little wave and then step outside onto the curb.

The warm evening air kisses my sweaty skin as I carry my mat to my car. The stunning sky shows off a vivid, beautiful spectrum of colors, reminding me of my mother. Mom always loved the setting sun. Her last request before she passed away three years ago was to open the curtains so she could watch the sunset. The universe didn't let her down. That sunset was the most beautiful spectacle I've ever seen, and thinking about it brings tears to my eyes.

"In you go," I say, tossing my yoga mat into the back seat. Then I take my spot behind the wheel.

My car purrs as I pull onto the street and head toward my house. The ride is smooth, and with the radio off, it's a nice bubble of peace. It's a nice change from the chaos of the office this afternoon. Between a shooting involving Sebastian in California, a routine audit from an outside accounting firm, and Theo suddenly *not* getting to stay in the office, it was tense and hectic for everyone. The only bright spot was Troy bringing me lunch ... and three cookies because, apparently, there was a sale.

I'm rarely eager to leave work. Today, I couldn't wait to get out the door.

My dash lights up moments before I hear my phone ring. I glance down and see my father's wife calling—my stepmom. Alexis isn't wicked like the stories always promise, but it's ... awkward. Sometimes I'm glad Mom missed this particular development in my life, but other times, I wish she was here to talk to about things like this. It can be hard to separate my emotions from logic and to look at things from different perspectives. Mom was great at that.

"This should be interesting," I mutter before pressing the button to answer. "Hey, Alexis."

"Hey, Dahlia. How are you?"

My stomach tenses as I attempt to decode her tone. She doesn't call often, but given the updates I caught on the news, who knows why she's calling today.

Alexis Dallo is, by all accounts, a likable person. She seems smitten with my dad, and he's equally taken with her. Sure, she might be young—only three years older than me, something I learned after seeing her thirtieth birthday pictures on Social a few months ago—but love is love, and she's been nothing but kind to me. We wouldn't exactly be friends if it wasn't for her marriage to my father, but we can handle the roles we have just fine.

"I'm hanging in there," I say, squinting into the light. "How are you guys doing over there?"

"We're hanging in there, too."

Her voice is heavy with exhaustion, and my heart hurts for her.

My coping mechanism regarding the whole trial has been to avoid it —to *not* think about it. Luckily, I have a lifetime of habits on my side. I'm not used to thinking about my father, so although I've worried about him, blocking the hoopla from my mind hasn't been an impossible challenge. That can't be true for Alexis.

"Your father has wanted to get ahold of you for the past couple of days. It's all I've heard—*I need to check on Dahlia.*" She laughs. "By the time he gets a moment to himself, it's late at night, and he doesn't want to disturb you. He winds up passing out anyway, the poor man."

Even without the trial, it's been established that my father is a hard worker. He took his father's successful business and increased it one hundredfold. Articles are written about him. I'm sure his confidence and work ethic were qualities that attracted Mom to him in the first place. A part of me wishes he would've applied some of that determination to being a father much earlier in life, but no amount of wishing will change that now.

"How's he doing?" I ask.

"He's a trooper. He's confident this will all be resolved. I don't know if he's telling me that to make me feel better or if he really believes it, but he's marching forward."

"I feel bad that I can't be there more for you. But he told me to stay away and—"

"Oh, Dahlia, no. Please don't feel that way. You're doing the right thing. Joe worries himself to death that you'll get drawn into this mess, and if you stay away, that's one less thing he has to deal with. I'm sorry if that sounds harsh."

An awkwardness fills the line between my stepmother and me.

It's such an odd relationship. This woman could be my sister. And, to make it even weirder, she's known my dad longer than I have. No amount of kindness will ever make this feel ... normal.

"It doesn't sound harsh," I say, turning left.

"There's so much happening behind the scenes, and this is just ... the accusations are wild. I hope they're ready to be sued once this is over and it's proven to be a witch hunt to steal your father's assets."

"The attorneys are optimistic then?"

"Yes. Our team feels confident that things are going well. Our attorneys are filing motions and poking holes into the prosecution's case. They're definitely earning their money."

Good thing Dad has enough of it, then.

I drive down the street and into my driveway. "Will you please tell my father I'm thinking of him?"

"Absolutely. He asked me to let you know you're always in his thoughts."

"It was very nice of you to call. Thank you."

Alexis sighs. "Okay, I need to go. I'm glad you're doing well, and I'll pass along your message to Joe. Take care."

"You, too."

"Of course. Goodbye."

"Goodbye."

I sigh, grab my stuff, and exit the car. I sort my emotions as I get to the front door.

It occurs to me that Alexis's call summarizes our relationship. It's friendly and thoughtful—she didn't have to call or tell me anything. It's also forced and abrupt. But maybe that's just normal in this *anything but normal* situation. We're all trying our best. This can't be easy for her either.

I smile and open the door. *At least I had my mother. I had the best. I can't ask for anything more.* I toss my bag on the requisite chair and kick off my shoes. My body begs for a hot bath while my head cries for a glass of wine.

Wine wins.

I head to the kitchen. I'm reaching for a glass when my phone vibrates in my other hand.

> Troy: My expense report has been uploaded to the system.

I sink against the counter, my hip digging into the square edge, and type a message back.

> Me: I didn't even have to ask. <heart-eyed emoji>

> Troy: It's integral to my employment.

> Me: You don't want to admit you're getting trained by me. Slowly but surely, you're getting right where I want you. <evil laugh emoji>

> Troy: And where might that be?

Heat flames my cheeks as I reread his message. Either I'm reading that wrong or Troy is developing a sense of humor.

How do I answer this? I certainly can't say that I'd like him any way he'd take me—pinning me against a wall, throwing my legs around his neck, beneath me as I bounce on his cock.

> Me: I can't tell you that. <shushing face emoji>

> Troy: Why not?

> Me: Because then it won't be any fun.

I lift my gaze to pick up my glass when my sight settles on something else.

Troy's response buzzes in my palm, but I don't read it.

A slow shudder runs the length of my spine as I examine the refrigerator magnets. The two squirting ones have been moved to the bottom.

Burt didn't touch them yesterday. They were in the correct spot when he left after dinner. And they were where they were supposed to be when I left for work. I grabbed a bottle of water for the drive and would've noticed if they were out of place. It would've bothered me.

But it didn't. *Because they were in the right spot.*

I glance over my shoulder as the hairs on the back of my neck stand on end.

Did Burt come here while I was gone? I mull that over. It's the simplest answer, but he's never done that before. He certainly doesn't have a key. I bite my bottom lip. *Maybe he thought I was home, and I'd left the door unlocked.*

I swallow past the lump in my throat.

My skin prickles with anticipation as I swipe off my text app and call Burt. Each ring feels like a lifetime. Thankfully, it only takes three lifetimes for him to pick up.

"Hey, sweet pea," he says. "Are you calling to tell me you didn't eat that chocolate cake in the fridge and I can have it?"

"Hey, Burt." I suck in a quick, hot breath. "That's not why I was calling, actually. I have a really weird question for you. You didn't come by my house today by any chance, did you?"

"Nope. Why?"

"Just ... No reason. I was just curious."

"Was I supposed to?"

I shake my head, even though he can't see me. "No. You weren't. I just thought maybe you needed something and just came in. The magnets that you always mess with were moved. I know you didn't move them last night."

"Magnets? What are you talking about?"

"The magnets ..." Troy's texts buzz again. "You know, the two magnets on my refrigerator that you like to move around."

"What?" He chuckles. "Sweet pea, I don't touch your magnets. You warn me every time not to."

My throat narrows, and I still.

Is he screwing with me?

Burt has moved the magnets three times over the past couple of weeks ... *hasn't he?* I rack my brain to remember why I assumed it was Burt but can't remember.

If it's not him, then who is it?

My heart drums against my ribs.

"Did you happen to see anyone here today?" I ask, my words falling fast. "Was anyone here at all?"

"Not this afternoon, but your friend Morgan just pulled up."

"She did? Just now?"

"Yeah. *Hi, Morgan,*" he calls out.

My breath comes in and out rapidly. "Burt, I need to go. Thanks for your help."

"Anytime."

I end the call and race to the front door, pulling it open as Morgan's knuckle is poised to knock. She takes me in and moves back.

"Are you okay?" she asks.

"I don't know."

"What's going on? I just stopped by on the off chance you were here. I thought we could grab dinner, but I feel like I just interrupted something."

"Come in," I say, allowing her to enter my house. I shut the door softly.

Suddenly, everything feels off. The oxygen in the room decreases, and energy flows through the walls. I feel like an outsider in my home.

I steady myself. "I'll preface this by saying I've had a long day. And Mallory had us doing hot yoga today, which has messed with my brain before."

"*Okay.*"

I square my shoulders to hers. "I might be losing my mind, I don't know, but I think ..."

It feels ridiculous to say it. My brain's going too fast to get a grip

55

on my thoughts. Everything I start to say feels like a terrible over-reaction.

"What's going on?" Morgan asks. "You're freaking me out."

"I'm sorry. I just ... Do you know the two squirting magnets you got me for my birthday?"

She nods.

"They keep moving around on my fridge. Both of them. I assumed it was Burt because he'd been here right before I noticed it the last three times. But I just got home from work, and they were moved. I know they were in the right places this morning."

Her brows pull together. "Did he come in while you were gone?"

"He says he didn't. And I don't think he would've."

"And you're sure they didn't just slide?"

"Yes. I keep them in a certain spot, and if they slid, the ones around them would have to move. They'll be in the opposite upper corner of the fridge. Someone is moving them."

She takes a deep breath. "Could it be Freddy?"

Fuck.

"Did you give him a key to your house?" she asks carefully.

"Yeah. I did. I mean, I got it back, but he could've made a copy of it."

"Who else could it be?"

I sigh, partially relieved there's a logical answer—and partially sick from it, too. "No one. It has to be him. He's been texting and calling me every day, wanting another chance. Or he wants to come by and look for his sunglasses, or he thinks he left his gold chain here. Maybe he's just trying to intimidate me or make me think I need him."

Morgan looks around, then swipes the bottle of wine off the counter. "I'm bringing this. You're going to get your stuff for work tomorrow and stay the night at my house."

"That's not necessary."

She laughs. "Oh, *it is*. If Freddy's coming in here, you don't know what he could do. You broke up with the guy because he was doing cocaine in your bathroom."

Fair point.

"Stay the night with me," Morgan says. "Tomorrow, you can call a locksmith and get your locks changed. Have Burt keep a lookout. See if you can file a police report to have it on record."

I nod.

My adrenaline begins to subside, and rational thought takes back over. While creepy and wrong on all levels, it's just Freddy being a dick. He's moving my magnets to bother me.

I bite my lip.

What if it's not just moving my magnets ...

My stomach churns as I fight myself not to go there.

"Come on," Morgan says. "Let's get your stuff and get out of here."

"Okay."

I take a step when my phone vibrates. There are several missed texts spanning the last twenty minutes. I groan, hoping to hell it's not Freddy blowing me up. I'm not sure I can handle that right now.

> Troy: It would be more fun if I knew your endgame.

> Troy: I take it you disagree.

> Troy: Are you okay?

> Troy: Dahlia?

> Troy: I know I'm not entitled to a response within a certain timeframe, but just let me know you're okay.

> Troy: For fuck's sake.

"Who is that?" Morgan has the baseball bat I keep by the door angled over her shoulder.

"Troy."

She grins. "You know, this is his specialty. Maybe you should ask him for advice."

"Absolutely not."

"Why not? This seems like the most authentic way for you to get that man over here."

"That crosses a line from professional to personal."

"I think—"

"*No*," I say emphatically. "This is just Freddy being a jerk. I won't embarrass myself by telling him my ex is moving my magnets around." I roll my eyes and start up the steps. "That even sounds silly."

"It's silly until it's not."

"That's why I'll call the police and file a report. I need to put my phone on the charger first."

We clear the upstairs with the bat positioned for a grand slam. Then I head to my bedroom and plug my phone into the wall. Before I look up the number for the police department, I open my texts again.

> Me: Hey. Sorry about that. My friend Morgan showed up. I'm fine.

> Troy: Good to hear.

> Me: I'll see you in the morning.

> Troy: Good night.

For once, I'm too preoccupied to taunt him with emoji. I make a police report instead.

Chapter Seven

Dahlia

There's not enough coffee in the world to get me through today.

I yawn, filling my mug before I even bother going to my office. I had a cup at Morgan's before I left for work. But between her house's subzero temperature, her cat clawing at my bedroom door all night, and the neighbor's car alarm waking me up at four o'clock, the single cup didn't touch my level of exhaustion.

And that doesn't factor in the bad dreams I had when I did manage to close my eyes for more than five minutes.

"Good morning," Becca says, breezing into the break room. She's looking smart in her simple black skirt and white button-down. A pale pink bow is delicately wrapped around her ponytail that matches the distinct corded bracelet she wears every single day. She's effortlessly chic. *And rested.* "How are you?"

Anxious. Tired. Irritable. "I'm great. You?"

"I'm good." She pours herself a cup of coffee, too. "I was talking

59

to one of my friends from Kismet Beach on the way to work this morning. That always makes for a good start to the day."

"It is always nice to talk to old friends. Kismet Beach. That's in Florida, right?"

"Yeah." She takes a sip. "I'm originally from Texas, but I moved to Indiana. I lived there for a while and then moved to Florida."

"How in the world did you wind up in Savannah?"

"Foxx Carmichael, actually," she says. "He's from Kismet Beach. I was friends with his brothers' girlfriends. Long story short, he got me a job here." She pauses, wrinkling her nose. "Sort of. It's complicated."

"Of course it is. Foxx is involved," I say, laughing.

"Exactly." She heads for the door. "Have a good day, Dahlia."

"You, too, Becca."

Her ponytail swishes as she moves down the hallway.

"Let's get this day started, shall we?" I mumble, exiting the break room. I wave to Ford's assistant, Hoda, and then step inside my office.

I flip on the lights and set my things on my desk. Leftover adrenaline lingers in my body, making my mind work faster ... and less efficiently. I can't remember what I need to do first this morning, nor if I have any meetings or conference calls.

I log on to my computer as my cell phone rings. I glance down and don't know the number.

Do I pick it up? Or let voicemail answer?

I run through a series of possibilities, deciding at the last minute to answer. It could be the police checking to see if I got the form they were emailing me to sign and return. Besides, there's nothing to be shaken up over. It was just Freddy, and he's an asshole but harmless.

"Hello?" I say, my tone nice and even.

"Hi, Dahlia. I hope I'm not interrupting anything."

My heartbeat quickens. I spring to my feet and close my office door. Looks like he needed to change his number ... again.

"Hi, Dad." The name still tastes foreign on my tongue, yet I like it. "How are you? It's good to hear your voice."

"I've been meaning to call, sweetheart." He sighs. "That sounds like an excuse. I suppose it *is* an excuse."

"You have a lot going on. I'm pretty sure I can forgive you this time."

He chuckles. "Your mother did an amazing job raising you, Dahlia. You are such a kind, smart young woman. I'm so proud to call you my daughter even though I had nothing to do with how wonderful you are."

I grin. "Thank you."

It's so weird to think about my parents together, and what that interaction looked like ... and what it could've looked like between the three of us. People change over time, but I think we could've been happy as a family. I lament the fact that we never tried to be one.

"One day, after this circus is behind me, you and I will have some time to ourselves. Just the two of us," he says. "We haven't had a chance to do that."

"No, we haven't. I'd like that. A lot."

"Me, too. So how are things with you? How's work going?"

For a brief, fleeting moment, I consider telling him about Freddy and the intrusion of my privacy but decide against it. It's not really important, and he has bigger, heavier fish to fry. Besides, it's not really how we interact yet. He hasn't been in my life long enough for me to consider offering him insight into certain aspects of my world—especially when they involve boyfriends.

"Things are going great," I say instead. "We're between projects right now, so it's the calm before the storm. I call it housekeeping because I'm making sure all of our paperwork is up to date and our plans for the next project are approved. Those kinds of things."

"Landry Security better watch out. I might steal you for myself with such exceptional organizational skills."

I laugh. "I really like it here. They're very good to me."

"That's what I like to hear. Do you need anything? I know I'm preoccupied with this legal nightmare right now, but if you need anything at all, I want to know. I want to help."

I close my eyes and take a minute to absorb the warmth flowing through my veins.

How can this man be guilty of all of the things leveled against him?

Money makes people do crazy things, and it's true, I suppose, that Joseph Dallo, the businessman, could be vastly different from Joseph Dallo, the father. And his kindness to me might simply be based out of regret for not being in my life for so long. But I'm grateful to have him in my life, and I have a very difficult time imagining that this man is the same man laundering money for a cartel.

"I don't need anything right now. Thanks for asking, though."

"Of course." He sighs again. "I've taken up enough of your time this morning. I keep trying to find a time to call you that is appropriate, but it never seems to work out. So this morning I thought, I'm going to call my daughter and check on her. If she can't answer, I'll leave a message."

"I do love a good voice message," I say, laughing. "But I'm really glad you called. And thank you for having Alexis check in with me yesterday."

"I wanted you to know you're always on my mind."

"That's really nice. I think about you, too, and hope you're well."

"We'll get through this. I promise." He takes a breath. "Take care, sweetheart. You have my assistant Frances's number, don't you?"

"Yes."

"If you need anything, call her. I may have to keep my distance, but I can make things happen."

"Thank you. I will. Have a good day," I say.

"You, too. Talk soon."

"Goodbye."

I collapse back into my chair and let out the deepest breath known to man. The movement settles my heartbeat a bit.

I take a moment to get myself together. Waking up in someone else's house and being reminded that your personal space has been tainted sent me into another round of uneasiness. I'm less fearful than yesterday—I've accepted that Freddy's to blame. But that doesn't fix how exposed I feel, and I hope that feeling doesn't linger long.

I just have to get through it.

Even if it takes boatloads of caffeine to do it.

My coffee is still hot when I take a quick sip and get started on my work. Nothing exploded or fell apart during the night, which always makes for an easier morning. I click on my personal email, hoping the detective remembered to send me the form I need to sign, and type in my username. *I need to get this over and done with so I don't have to think about it all day.*

"Hey."

I jump, looking toward the door. Troy stands with a mug in his hand and a curious look on his handsome face.

"Hi," I say, letting my gaze linger on his exposed forearms thanks to his rolled-up sleeves. "I didn't hear you knock."

"Because I didn't."

I shake my head and go back to my computer. "I thought we discussed this."

"We did. Theo knocks. I don't."

I scoff, typing in my password.

"Are you going to tell me what's going on with you?" he asks, sitting across from me.

"Nothing is going on with me."

"You're lying."

Yes, I am. But I'm not discussing this with you. I try my password again. "You're just mad that I made you wait too long last night for a response. Too bad. I was busy. Get over it."

"I know something was going on last night, Doll."

"What are you, some kind of seer now?"

He sips his drink, watching me over the brim with zero amusement.

"Fine. For the record, something *was* going on," I say. "My friend Morgan stopped by, and we were doing a little ... investigation."

63

"About what?"

I smile at him. "You know as well as I do that security issues are confidential." I laugh at the look on his face. "*Aw.* That doesn't feel as good when you're on that side of things, does it?"

"It's a little different when I'm asking about you and your friend, and you wanted me to give you the inside scoop on a pop star's ex-boyfriend."

"Oh, it's a lot different." I laugh. "You had tea to spill. Morgan and I just carried a bat around my house."

"And why did you have a bat?"

"I used to play softball," I say, knowing damn well and good that's not the answer he was looking for. "Now, if you don't have a purpose for being here, I do have things to do today."

"So we're just going to pretend that everything was fine last night?"

I huff before staring at him. "I told you. *Everything* is *fine.*"

He smirks. "I do this for a living, you know. Watch people and notice when things are suspicious. And I'm really fucking good at it."

"Well, guess what, you burly little investigator? I'm fine. Nothing was going on. I wasn't scared."

"I didn't say you were scared. I asked if you're okay."

Shit. I retype in my password. This time, it works. "I'm getting annoyed."

"Be annoyed at yourself. You're the one Freudian slipping."

"That's not a thing."

"It's absolutely a thing."

"*Freudian slipping* is not a thing. It doesn't even sound like a thing." I skim my inbox—no email from the detective. I start to click out of the window when something catches my eye. "You're just mad you don't have all the answers."

If he answers, I don't hear him. I'm focused on a message sent a few hours ago.

My blood runs ice cold.

White noise crashes over my ears as a shaky hand presses the mouse and opens the email.

To: Lovelace, Dahlia
From: Me
Re: Safety Check

Run or die.
Don't alert the authorities, or I'll make the choice for you.

My body tenses as my spine stiffens. Nausea swirls at the base of my esophagus, threatening to gag me with bitter bile. Troy's voice registers faintly over the blood rushing through my body as my trembling finger opens the attachment.

Oh my God.

I push away from my desk, clasping my hand over my mouth. My breath stalls in my lungs.

"Dahlia?" Troy asks.

I rip my gaze away from the terrifying images on the screen and bring them to him.

As soon as our eyes meet, he jumps to his feet.

My eyes fill with hot tears. I try to speak, but I don't know what to say. I can't find my voice through the shock ... and terror.

"What the fuck is going on?" he asks, his tone hard.

"Troy ... I ... I don't know."

My voice breaks.

He storms around my desk without an invitation and stands behind me. His energy rushes off him, smashing me in the back as he takes in the photographs displayed on my computer screen.

The first picture is me at the grocery store a few weeks ago, picking out lemons for a new lemon sorbet recipe I found online. The second image was snapped at a pizzeria the night I met Morgan and her brother for dinner. Next is a shot of me on a walk in the park last weekend. The next one, of me in my shower two nights ago, is the one that chills me to the bone. It ends with a picture of me at Morgan's kitchen table last night.

"What the hell is this?" Troy asks, spinning my chair around so I'm facing him. He holds the armrests, caging me in. "Who sent that?"

I shake my head. "I don't know."

He looks at it again, his teeth clenched.

My brain scrambles, searching for an explanation. "My first guess is Freddy, considering last night—"

"What the fuck happened last night, Dahlia?" His jaw pulses as he stares at me.

He's phrased it as a question, but it's a statement. *An order.* And, this time, it feels relevant to answer.

"Last night, I realized someone was in my house when I wasn't."

"*What?*"

I gulp, staring up at Troy. His eyes are blazing.

"Last night," I say, struggling to form words under his scrutiny. "I realized last night that someone has been in my house on and off for the past couple of weeks."

"You realized this last night?"

"Yes."

"And you didn't call me?"

I wipe my palms down my skirt and breathe.

"I should've been your first fucking call," he says, shoving away from the chair.

The movement breaks the moment, and I exhale sharply.

"Call *you?*" I jump to my feet. "Why? Because my ex-boyfriend has been sneaking into my house and moving around my magnets? You want me to call you for *that?*"

"Abso-*fucking*-lutely."

"I called the police and filed a report."

He takes a few steps back. "Looks like they're really on top of it, doesn't it?"

I want to argue with him. I want to explode, letting loose some of the energy making me shake.

Someone's been watching me. And now they're threatening to kill me.

"Come on," Troy says, heading for the door. His tone's not to be messed with.

"Where are we going?"

He jerks the door open and waits for me to comply. "Let's go."

Run or die.

"Troy, I need to think. I need to figure this out," I say, hysteria rising in my voice. "I need to call the police, I think. I don't know. What do I do? Do I leave? Do I run?" I clamp a hand on my stomach. "*Oh God.*"

"Hey."

I suck in a lungful of air and look at him through the tears in my eyes.

"I got you," he says, his voice softer than before. His eyes shine. "You're not in this alone."

His kind, stupid words cause a solitary tear to roll slowly down my cheek.

"I feel like I might panic," I say, swaying on my feet.

"Then panic."

"But isn't that like rule number one in security? Don't panic?"

"You can panic because I won't." He motions for me to go to him. And I do. "Now, let's go."

Troy's palm lays lightly on the small of my back, guiding me down the hallway.

"You're not in this alone."

For the first time in two days, I don't feel like I'm one hard breeze away from being knocked to the ground.

I glance at Troy. His fingers flex against my back.

And if I am thrown down, I'm pretty sure he'll pick me up.

Chapter Eight

T roy

I keep my eyes glued to Ford's office at the end of the hall.

The pictures in Dahlia's email are seared into my mind. As disturbing as it is to know someone was stalking her, it's easier to think about them than the fear in her eyes.

There are so many things I want to say and more things I want to do. I want to know why she didn't call me last night and how long this has been going on.

Who the fuck is this walking dead man?

I struggle to contain my rage. It takes everything I have not to explode and find the fucker who's behind this.

But I don't.

There's a time for calm and a time for war. I need to be patient.

Someone will pay for this. And I'll be the one to ring them up.

"*Hey,*" Dahlia whispers, coming to an abrupt halt. She looks at me with an unguarded fear that pierces my heart. "What are we doing? I'm just following you down the hall like a puppy."

The hysteria swimming in her eyes earlier has faded, and I can tell she's getting her wits about her again.

"We need to talk to Ford," I say.

"But the email said not to alert the authorities."

I pause and nod at Becca as she returns to her office. I wait for her door to close before I speak.

"The email is meant to intimidate you. You're right. You don't want to put this on a billboard until we get a handle on it and ..." I stop short of saying *murder the motherfucker who's behind this.* "And neutralize the threat."

Her lips twitch. "That's not what you were going to say."

"You aren't prepared for what I was going to say."

The air between us grows thicker. *Hotter.* Between her doe eyes and my aching need to protect her, there are too many layers of added danger to this already precarious situation.

"Ford needs to know," I say, circling us back to solid ground. "No person in this country is more equipped or capable of handling this situation."

"Are you sure?"

"Yes."

"Would this be your advice if I were your mother?"

I blink.

"That's what people say to doctors to get them to tell them the truth," she says. "They ask if the patient was their mother and if they'd recommend the treatment. So that's what I'm asking you. If I were your mother, would this be your advice?"

I resist the urge to touch the side of her face. Instead, I bite back a confession on the tip of my tongue and answer her question. "Yes."

Her shoulders straighten, and she lifts her chin. She inhales a shaky breath. "Okay."

My knuckles rap against Ford's door. Lincoln opens it almost immediately.

Dahlia's eyes snap to mine.

"Give us one second, Lincoln, please," I say.

He looks between us and then nods. The door shuts softly.

"Hey," I say, loud enough for only Dahlia to hear. I want her to be empowered—not to feel like her life is out of her control. The last thing she needs is to walk into a room with three men and feel like she has no say in what happens to her. "You weren't expecting Lincoln. I wasn't either. He's like a bad penny that keeps turning up."

A faint smile touches her lips.

"If you aren't comfortable discussing this in front of Lincoln, we'll wait until he leaves," I say. "This is your decision. You're in the driver's seat. I'm more than willing to take the steering wheel, but just tell me what you want."

She hiccups a breath and holds it. "I don't know what I want. I'm scared, Troy."

My hands clench at my sides to keep from pulling her to me. As hard as that is, I know it's about to get harder because I have no other choice. "Do you trust me?"

"I trust you with my life, and as ironic as it is, that's what we're dealing with here."

"Now isn't the time for jokes."

She grins a wobbly smile. "I was going to tell you to let me live my life, but that probably won't go over well either, huh?"

I narrow my eyes.

"Sorry," she says, attempting to wipe her features clean. "It's either make a joke or cry hysterically, and I'm an ugly crier. I also think I'm in shock right now."

I open the door and guide her in before me. It snaps closed behind us.

Ford's hands are folded on his desk, and he has a curious look on his face. Lincoln leans against a drawing table near the window, holding a cup of coffee. Surprisingly, there's no humor anywhere to be found.

"We have a situation," I say.

"What's going on?"

Dahlia looks up at me and shakes her head, silently requesting I speak for her.

"Last night, Dahlia discovered someone has been breaking into her house when she's not home," I say, the words falling flat.

Ford's brows arch. "How long has this been going on?"

"I'm not sure," Dahlia says. "A few weeks, I think."

"Did we change her locks?" Ford asks me. "Sweep her place for surveillance equipment?"

"Dahlia didn't tell me until this morning," I say.

Lincoln flinches.

"I called the police and then stayed the night at a friend's," she says. "This morning, a locksmith's going to my house. My neighbor Burt is going to meet them there."

"Do you have any idea who was breaking in?" Ford asks.

I hold up a hand. "We haven't even gotten to the fun part yet."

Ford's face sobers.

"She received an email this morning," I say.

"What kind of an email?" Ford asks.

I glance down at Dahlia. She's wary. Without thinking, I again place my hand on the small of her back. Just like before, she immediately relaxes a little.

I don't know what to think about this discovery—or if I want to think about it. Ever.

Dahlia turns back to Ford. "The email said that I should run or die." She shudders against my palm. "It had pictures attached that show me at different places over the past month or so."

Lincoln sets his mug on the table.

"I'm not sure what to do," she says, glancing at the three of us. "It said not to tell the authorities or whoever it is will kill me. I think that's what it meant. And I don't think it's a joke because of the pictures." She tries to smile. "What am I supposed to do? Leave? Never come back? Do I walk around for the rest of my life knowing someone is out there ... *watching me?*"

Ford stands, straightening his tie. "Don't panic."

71

"Troy said I could, and I'm teetering on the edge. It might be a relief to spiral into the abyss."

Ford looks at me, and I shrug.

"I was kidding," Dahlia says. "Can you guys not take a joke?"

"Do you have any thoughts on who might be behind this?" Ford asks, refocusing. "Is there anyone upset with you? Anyone who would want to hurt you?"

"I have an ex-boyfriend, Freddy. We broke up because he has a drug problem. Something I didn't put together until it was too late."

"Has he been coming around? Calling?" Ford asks, jotting notes on a pad of paper. "Threatening you?"

"Yes. Not really threatening me, just saying he can't live without me. I thought it was probably him breaking into my house. But I doubt he'd threaten to kill me. We weren't *that* serious."

I clear my throat. "Whoever was breaking into the house was also involved in the pictures. One photo was of her in her bathroom."

Dahlia's jaw drops. "I didn't think of that."

"All right. I'll have additional questions, but for now, let's get a plan together," Ford says.

I start to speak, but Dahlia cuts me off.

"*No*. Ford, no." She shakes her head adamantly. "You do not have to do this."

"Do what, exactly?" he asks.

"This isn't your problem. You're not even supposed to know about it." She grips the back of a leather chair that faces his desk. "I'm going to call the police. Then I'll go home, get a few things, and leave town."

As if Ford's waiting for my reaction, he turns to me with an expectant look.

There's only one solution to this. While it might make things messier in the long run, and I wish to hell there was another answer because this is going to kill me, I trust no one else. It has to be me.

I nod and answer his unspoken question. "Vacation."

Lincoln walks toward us. "I have a house on Kiawah Island. You can't even get on the island without credentials. There are roaming security guards, gatehouses, and then I have my own security system, of course."

"Jason Brewer owes me a favor," Ford says, taking his phone out of his pocket. "I'll borrow a Brewer Air plane. You'll be there in a couple of hours. You can land at the executive airport and take a car to the island."

Dahlia scoffs. "While you wrap up your vacation plans, I'm going to my desk to make some calls." Her eyes widen in disbelief. "I don't know if this is my resignation, Ford, or if ... yeah. I don't know."

Ford chuckles. Lincoln grins. I look at the ceiling because I know her better than they do. *She's gonna be pissed.*

"I'm glad you guys think this is funny," she says, irritated.

Ford comes around the corner of his desk. "You're not resigning, Dahlia. You're going on a paid vacation."

Her forehead wrinkles.

Ford looks at me.

Sure. Let me deliver the news.

"Do you know how I didn't know if I was going to Laina's or taking a vacation?" I ask.

She crosses her arms over her chest. "Yeah."

"I chose a vacation."

"Good for you."

"And you're going with me."

She takes a step back, her eyes wide. "*What?*"

Lincoln chuckles, a shit-eating grin plastered on his face. If this weren't a serious conversation, I'd tell him to fuck off.

"I'm not going on a vacation with you," she says, laughing in disbelief. "Have you not heard what I just said? Someone's threatening to kill me, guys. *Kill me.* I have to leave."

"You are leaving," I say. "With me."

"You are out of your mind, Castelli."

"Quite possibly."

She throws her hands up and turns to Ford. "You can't be serious.

73

I don't know who's after me. I don't know when I can come back. You can't pay me for … who knows how long. And what about Troy? You have stuff for him to do."

"This is, at the end of the day, your decision," I say, as much as it pains me. "But if you don't go with me, I'm going to have to follow you around. And while I'm sure that would be entertaining, it would be a lot easier and more comfortable to let me take you to Lincoln's house until Ford figures this out."

"Oh, so you're gonna stalk me, too?"

"Yes."

She opens her mouth, but nothing comes out. She just stares at me.

"Dahlia, I wish you would've called one of us last night," Ford says.

"He doesn't mean me," Lincoln says. "I'm not good in these situations."

Ford shakes his head. "But now that we know what's going on, we'll get to the bottom of it. In the meantime, we're going to keep you safe."

"I can't ask you to do that."

"You don't have to," I say, silently begging her to challenge me. "It's done."

She holds my gaze as Ford lists action points.

"I'll have Hoda get you a new phone," he says. "Turn yours off before you leave the office. Forward me the email you received. If you want, I can have someone from the office accompany a friend or a neighbor to your house to get a few things for you. We'll have them sent to you tonight. Don't tell anyone where you're headed. If asked, say you're taking a work trip and don't know when you'll return. Try to keep it vague."

Dahlia nods, her eyes still on mine. The longer she watches me, the less fear I can see in her eyes.

"Talk to as few people as you can," Ford says. "We need you off the grid as much as possible."

"I got her," I say, returning Dahlia's ghost of a smile. "Just get us out of here."

"I'll call Jason now," Ford says. "Lincoln, is everything good to go at your place?"

Lincoln clears his throat. "Yeah. It's good. I should let you know, though, that we've been renovating. There's only one working bedroom at the moment."

Oh. Fuck.

Dahlia sucks in a quick breath.

"But I'm sure you'll figure it out," he says, flinching when Ford fires him a look. "*What?*"

"One last thing," Ford says carefully. "You mentioned your ex and that makes sense. But do you think this could have anything to do with your father?"

Dahlia's face darkens, her chest rising and falling. She turns slowly to Ford.

"I know you must think this is related to him," she says slowly, having told our boss about the parental situation shortly after she found out. "But I don't. He has no motive. We've established a pretty good rapport."

"He might not have a motive," Ford says. "But the cartels might. Someone he does business with might. There's a lot of activity surrounding your father. I know you know that."

Lincoln's brows pull together, but he stays quiet. *For once.*

Dahlia takes in a shaky breath. "I feel really bad that you're getting involved in this."

"You're a part of our family," Ford says. "We won't let anything happen to you. I know Troy will have your back."

She looks at me from the corner of her eye. I stand as stoically as possible.

"Troy, if you need anything from home, grab it now," Ford says. "Dahlia, do you have anyone that can get anything you need from your house?"

"Yes. My friend Morgan."

"Okay. Let's get with Hoda and make those arrangements," Ford says. "We'll have you out of here as soon as we can."

Ford and Lincoln chat quietly, leaving Dahlia and me a moment to talk.

"Hey," I say, pulling her attention my way. "I'll be back in a little bit. Is there anything you want me to grab while I'm out?"

She looks around the room, unanchored. "Troy, I don't know. I'm overwhelmed."

"It's going to be okay. I'm with you every step of the way."

The smile on her face sets off a myriad of emotions through me. On the one hand, the consolation in her features settles me. On the other hand, the mere fact that she's dealing with this lights a fire deep in my soul that might be the death of me.

If she doesn't kill me first.

Chapter Nine

Dahlia

With my eyes closed, I lean my head against the side window, relishing the warmth of the sun caressing my skin. *Did I apply sunscreen this morning?* I have no clue. It feels like a lifetime ago.

The day has been an absolute blur. Between arranging for Morgan to meet Theo at my apartment to gather a few of my things without telling her why but insisting everything is absolutely fine, calling Burt and letting him know I'll be gone for a while and asking him to keep an eye on my house, having long, hard conversations with Ford and the police, and boarding a private jet, it's been a hell of a day.

The only silver lining to the flurry of activity is that I've worked out some of my feelings. It turns out that when you go through things in explicit detail, a cathartic response follows. And when Ford Landry makes it his mission to find out who's threatening you, there's a sense of security that comes along with it.

I glance over my shoulder.

And when a gorgeous, gray-eyed bad boy in a suit demands to whisk you off to an island to keep you safe—life could be worse.

Troy catches me watching him. I wait for a smile, a grin, or a smirk. Instead, he returns to the winding road leading to Kiawah Island.

"You've been quiet," I say as we cross a bridge.

There's been nothing but swamps, water, and vegetation for a long time. I'd think he was taking me to the middle of nowhere, except there's been a steady stream of cars in both directions.

"I didn't figure you wanted to talk," he says.

"Me? Not want to talk? It's like you don't even know me."

This gets me a half of a smile. "You've had a lot of shit thrown at you today. I wanted to give you space."

I shift in my seat, ready to get out of the car.

Troy hasn't said a whole lot since we left Landry Security a few hours ago. He's been on his phone off and on, and I've made a point not to listen. Not that I could hear or understand him anyway. But I'm sure if I did catch pieces of his conversations, my anxiety would rise again, and if there's one thing I don't want, it's that.

"How much farther until we get there?" I ask.

"You just asked me that."

"I haven't asked since the airport."

"We'll be there when we get there."

I laugh. "I bet your dad said that a lot to you growing up. You had to be the kid who was a giant pain in the ass."

A shadow falls over his face. "Something like that."

Out of nowhere, the vegetation parts and a security guard station blocks the road in front of us. A road extends to the right, disappearing into a grove of trees as the pavement curves around a bend.

"There's a blue piece of paper in the glove compartment," Troy says, motioning toward the dash. "Can you grab it for me, please?"

"Sure." I fiddle with the button until I open it and find the pale blue piece of paper tucked inside the owner's manual. "Here you go."

He takes it and pulls up to the guard station. A man with a long mustache holds out his hand.

"How are you folks this afternoon?" the man asks, looking at the paper. He then inspects the car's VIN beneath the windshield wiper.

"We're good. You?" Troy asks.

"I'm here. That's about all I can say for today."

I grin. "I like your mustache."

The man leans down to see me more clearly. "Thank you, young lady." He hands Troy the blue paper. "Do you know where you're going?"

"I do," Troy says.

"Very well. Enjoy your visit."

"Thank you," I say, giving him a friendly wave.

Troy shakes his head as we pull through the gate.

"What are you shaking your head about?" I ask.

"We're here quietly, meaning the idea is to stay hidden in plain sight. That doesn't really work when you're chatting with the pilot on the plane, exchanging Black Friday tips with the lady at the airport, and complimenting a guy on his fucking mustache."

"Well, that mustache was cool as hell. The pilot was nice. And I don't gatekeep shopping tips." I cross my arms over my chest and admire the luscious green golf course on either side of the road. "Just so you know, I was going to ask how much longer until we're there, but I stopped myself."

We approach another guard shack, and the blue paper process is repeated. This time, I don't mention the guy's neat silver-y beard.

We enter what appears to be a neighborhood full of very, *very* expensive homes. Trees tower over the road, casting shade on the car and instantly bringing the temperature down a few degrees.

Troy's forearm flexes as he turns the steering wheel into the driveway of the largest home at the end of the narrow street. Foliage from the trees and shrubs blocks a direct view of the house from the road. But as we pull farther into the driveway, all breath leaves my body.

My jaw drops. *"Oh, my gosh.* We're staying *here?"*

"Lincoln Landry does nothing small."

"You know, I've always suspected that."

Troy glares at me as he parks the car, but I'm too preoccupied with the house to care.

A two-story, villa-style home sits proudly in front of us. The light brown stucco is accented with a deep chocolatey color around the windows and trim. It somehow feels quaint and majestic at the same time.

The garage door opens, and we pull inside. It closes behind us.

"I guess if we have to leave our homes, at least we get to stay here, right?" I ask, climbing out of the car.

"It could be worse."

Troy types in a code onto a keypad. I smile at him as we step inside.

A small foyer is bright with cream-colored stone floors and almost pink-hued plaster walls that give the room a Mediterranean feel. Straight ahead is an arched doorway that leads to a patio. We turn to the left and enter the main living area.

Troy heads straight for a small room off the kitchen while I pause to take in the grandeur.

Windows line the wall facing me, showcasing a lush backyard full of tropical green plants and a pool. A chandelier hangs from the trayed ceiling over the center of a long table with leather bench-style chairs. The room opens on the left into a living area with oversized blue sofas and a ridiculous television. Pictures and baseball memorabilia are poised on built-in cabinets on either side and below the screen.

"Look at this kitchen," I say, running my fingertips along the island countertop. "Is Lincoln's wife a chef?"

"No clue," Troy says from around the corner.

"What are you doing?"

He comes back into view. "Checking the security system."

"Are we good?"

"We're good."

His shoulders drop, and he exhales slowly. For the first time today, I think he relaxes.

Suddenly, I'm aware we're alone. Troy and I are in this beautiful house, away from everyone and everything. And it's all for me.

My chest tightens. "Hey."

He lifts a brow.

"Thank you," I say. "I don't know if I've said that in my rambles today. You didn't have to do this, and I really appreciate it. I'm sure it's very inconvenient."

He stiffens again.

"But," I say, "you should be thanking me, too. I basically saved you from Laina Kelley. Talk about being a hero."

He tries not to show his amusement but fails.

"Come on," I say. "Let's see the upstairs."

"You don't find being in someone else's house awkward?"

"Actually, yes, I do." I grip the iron railing and lead him up the stairs. "But this is a once-in-a-lifetime opportunity to stay in a home that I'll never, ever be able to afford. So I might as well soak it up." She pauses. "Hell, I might be dead by the end of the day."

"There are a lot of possibilities over the next few days, but that's not one of them."

I blush, making sure I don't look at him. He probably meant that literally—and that's not how I took it.

We check out three emptied bedrooms to the right of the stairs. In one of them, a scaffold is set up as if a painting crew's about to start work. We go to the other side of the staircase and into a cozy bedroom with a white and blue bed, light-colored wood furniture, and an en suite.

"Look at that tub," I squeal. "I've dreamed of having one since I was a little girl. My mother and I watched a movie where the girl bathed in a tub like this. Mom thought it was the epitome of sophistication, and that idea has been implanted in my brain ever since."

"Does this make you a bath lover?"

"Yes. Absolutely. What's more luxurious than lying in a basin of hot, soapy, sweet-smelling water until it runs cold?"

His lips twitch.

"What?" I ask, curious. "What are you thinking?"

"Nothing."

"Tell me, Troy."

"Nothing," he says, chuckling. "You're right. A bath is the most luxurious thing in the world."

I stick a finger into the middle of his solid chest—regretting it as soon as I make contact.

A blast of energy shoots up my finger and frazzles every nerve in my body. Troy's eyes flash, but he recovers more quickly than I do. Still, I try to play it off by walking around him and into the massive walk-in closet.

"I like you agreeing with me," I say, hoping my voice doesn't betray me. "But not if you're making fun of me."

"I'd never do such a thing."

"Look at this," I say, pointing at an island in the closet that's bigger than most kitchen islands. "This is utterly ridiculous and the coolest freaking thing at the same time."

Troy shakes his head. "These people have more money than they know what to do with."

I hop onto the island and swing my feet back and forth. "What would you do if you had all this money?"

He shrugs.

"Come on," I say, taunting him. "What would you do? Would you buy a house like this? Would you buy a fancy car? Would you just travel the world and not have a care in the world?"

"I don't know. I guess I'd probably make sure Travis is set up for life and then take it day by day."

My heart squeezes at the look in his eyes when he mentions his brother.

Troy's said things about Travis here and there. I know his brother exists. I know they have dinner together sometimes. But I don't know anything deeper.

"Are you close with Travis?" I ask.

He nods.

"He's your only sibling, right?"

He nods again.

I smile. "We might be here a while. If you don't start talking, you'll have to listen to me, which usually irritates you."

"Excellent point." He gives me a crooked grin. "Trav is my only brother. We're pretty close. I don't see him every day or anything like that, but you know ..."

I hop off the counter. "He's really lucky to have you."

"Can I ask you something?"

"Sure."

"How do you stay so positive? Just a few hours ago, someone threatened to kill you. And instead of crying on the sofa or freaking the fuck out, you're ..." He shrugs. "*You.*"

He holds my gaze as I stare at him, internalizing his statement. The warmth of his words, the care in his tone—something I've only heard in this way a few times over the years—caresses my heart.

This is the side of Troy that I wish I knew better.

There's a weak spot, a soft underbelly, and he fights against it. He goes out of his way to prevent anyone from seeing him as anything but a hard-ass. *Why?*

"What else can I do?" I ask. "I could sit here and obsess over it and convince myself that my life is over. But what good would that do? And what if it's not even true? What if it's just Freddy being a prick? Do I let him win?" I grin. "I'm going to turn a lemon into lemonade and enjoy my time here. Even if it *is* with you."

He rolls his eyes, making me laugh.

"To be honest, I've been thinking about it all afternoon," I say. "And the more I mull it over, the more I think it's Freddy."

"Really?"

"Yeah. I do. This is a little sophisticated for him in a way. But, in a way, it's not. Who sends an email like that? Someone who's trying to scare me and upend my life, and the obvious answer is Freddy. Maybe he thinks it will drive me back to him. Who knows?"

Troy clears his throat. "That makes sense. But you do realize, and I'm not trying to scare you here, but there is the possibility that it's not him and someone else has an agenda, right?"

"Maybe." I walk to the small window and peer out. The view extends across the backyard to the sandy beach and beyond to the ocean. "Do you think I could go to the beach?"

"With me."

I laugh. "Do you think you're going everywhere I go?"

"No. *I know it.*"

"I'll be getting a bath this evening," I say, turning on my heel. The toe of my shoe catches on the rug, and I fly forward into Troy's arms. "*Oof.*"

My fingers splay against his chest. His right arm loops around my waist, holding me in place. His body is as hard as a rock, and once reality settles in, my knees weaken.

I've never been this close to this man, but I've imagined it a million times. It's better than the best daydream.

I lift my gaze to him, and the energy between us immediately shifts.

It's not just a daydream that ends with a sweet kiss. This is a setup for much, *much* more.

His eyes flash. His nostrils flare. His heartbeat is as rapid as mine.

I gulp a breath as he flexes his fingers against my waist.

The air between us ripples with tension. I'm pushed toward him and pulled away—trapped in a current of uncertainty that could go one of two ways.

I know the way I want it to go.

He searches my eyes as if looking for permission. I lift my chin.

Troy lowers his face toward mine ever so slowly. I hold my breath, desire pooling between my legs as he licks his lips.

Oh shit.

Troy's going to do this. *He's really going to do this.*

His hot breath dusts my lips, the heat of his mouth melting me from the inside out. I reach up, slipping my hand around the back of his neck, and feel his warm skin. Bolts of heat shoot through my fingertips at the connection. *I've wanted to touch him so many times. And now I get to ...*

I quiver, panting as he smirks—knowing he has me—and tugs me even tighter against him.

I smile, popping up on my toes to make contact ... when his phone rings.

My lungs release my breath in one long, heavy draw. Troy releases me and backs away. I sag against the wall, frazzled and mind blown. Uncertainty impregnates the air between us.

He brings his phone to his ear, never breaking eye contact. "Castelli."

His jaw sets as he listens to someone on the other end of the line. Finally, after what feels like forever, he rips his gaze away from mine and walks out of the room.

I almost yelp.

I almost yell, too.

Chapter Ten

T roy

      I bring the spoon to my lips and taste the sauce. *Not bad for canned garbage ingredients.*

The only thing I got from my mother that's worth a damn, aside from Travis, is her homemade sauce recipe. It came from her mother, my grandmother—a woman I never knew. In my mind, she was a robust, warm lady with a smile and a hug at the ready.

All the things my mother wasn't.

I take a step back and survey the scene. Steam rises from the stove. The oven light is on, keeping the garlic bread warm. Bits of onion and garlic litter the countertop, and an empty sauce jar sits by the sink. It's been a while since I cooked a decent meal, and by the looks of it, that's obvious.

After the call that saved me from making a huge fucking mistake in the closet, I searched for Dahlia to apologize. I found her asleep on the bed. It was no surprise and was a relief, really. The woman had to be exhausted. She's brave and strong, but the emotional toll of what happened today would weaken even the most seasoned person.

I pulled a blanket over her and came downstairs. Lincoln warned there was little to eat, and he was right, so I ordered a grocery delivery so we could have dinner.

Cooking took my mind off my fuckup in the closet. At least for a while.

I pick up my buzzing phone. "Castelli."

"Hey, Troy. It's Ford."

I set the spoon on a saucer. "How are things?"

"Theo found three cameras inside Dahlia's house, two of which had audio capabilities. He cut the power to the house before he went in, so whoever's behind it doesn't know we know."

Rage pours through me, making my skin feel too tight for my body.

"Did Theo leave them?" I ask.

"Yes. He had to. If we'd taken them down, they'd know something was amiss. There was a tracker on her car, too."

"What the fuck, Ford? Who the hell is behind this?"

I turn the burners off and pace the room.

A part of me is furious and feels worthless for not being there to help find the person or people behind this. The other part of me feels grateful to be here, ensuring no one touches Dahlia.

I rack my brain for any details we've missed or leads we haven't picked up on.

"I don't know yet," Ford says. "The puzzle pieces are ... interesting, to say the least."

"How?"

"Well, for starters, her father. Do you know how he came into her life? Or when? What prompted that? Joseph Dallo has a storied history and not for anything good. We can't rule him out. We can't rule out the people he's involved with either. There's a web of characters capable and willing to pull something like this. It's going to take a bit of time to sort through them. You know how it works."

"I don't know much about how Dallo came around. I'll see what I can find out."

87

"Do that. We've also been digging into her ex-boyfriend, Freddy Henke. Kid's a dipshit. Up until about a year ago, he was as clean as a whistle. He has a college degree in finance and comes from a good family. They seem to have disowned him after he got hooked on drugs last year. Dahlia was the only stable person in his life. Her neighbor said he saw Freddy drive by late last night, but he didn't stop."

I run a hand over my scalp. "What can I do from here?"

"Keep her out of here. You know the drill. Keep her out of harm's way and let us figure this out." He pauses. "What's she doing now?"

"Sleeping. She passed out a few hours ago."

"That will do her some good. Was everything good when you landed? Had Grey done a check of Lincoln's house?"

"Yeah. Grey had been here. He did a sweep of everything and rebooted all the systems just like we asked."

"Great. Okay, well, I was just checking in and seeing how things were going. If you need anything, give one of us a call. And Troy?"

"Yeah?"

Ford hesitates. "I don't know how to say this, so I'm just going to say it. We have things covered here. We're working every angle. So why don't you breathe a little? I know you're technically working, but you aren't monitoring concerts or your favorite adolescent fans. Surely, you can relax with one grown woman."

If you only knew ... "Sure."

"I mean it. Do your job but enjoy the time away. I have all the faith in the world that you can do both."

I stand straight. The silence in the room is unbearable.

There's a hitch to Ford's voice that hints at more than he's saying. *Or maybe I'm just self-conscious because I almost kissed Dahlia today like a selfish asshole.*

My palm sweats against the phone, and I shift my weight from one foot to the other.

I must get myself together. No more mistakes. She's my friend and my co-worker—*someone I've sworn to protect*—and I cannot cross that line. And I really can't cross it when she's going through so much. I won't be the guy who takes advantage of a woman in a situation like this. *Even if I want her with every fiber of my being.*

My stomach clenches.

"Need anything else?" I ask.

"No. That's it for now. Call me if you need anything, all right?"

"Talk to you later."

"Goodbye."

I end the call and set my phone on the counter beside the spoon. The edge of the phone smacks the end of the utensil, sending the dirty spoon flying through the air and smacking me in the side.

I look down to see red streaked down my shirt.

"Dammit," I mumble, stripping the fabric off and setting it next to the sink. Just as I reach for the dish soap, movement catches my eye.

Dahlia comes down the stairs, yawning.

My God.

Her hair's a mess. Her eyes are swollen. A crease is indented on the side of her cheek from how she lay in bed.

And I've never seen her *this* beautiful.

My heart skips a beat as I look at her, drinking her in as she stands at the base of the stairs.

I search her face, desperate to commit this to memory—the way she looks *and* the way it feels to be here with her right now.

Her gaze drags down my shoulders, over my chest, and across my abs. My skin tingles from the contactless contact. I itch to grab her, hold her, bury my face in her hair, and breathe her in.

But I don't. I can't. That would be stupid.

A soft smile graces her plump lips. It does things to me that I don't want to acknowledge. It makes my mind go places that aren't safe.

What have I gotten myself into?

"I smelled food," she says softly, walking to me.

"I was starving and thought you must be, too."

She holds a hand on her stomach. "Can you hear that? It's growling."

"Good thing I cooked, then."

She's surprised. "I didn't know you knew how to cook."

"There are lots of things about me that you don't know," I say.

She sits at a barstool across from me and yawns again. "You're right. I don't. Let's fix that."

"You just woke up. How about we eat before you start grilling me?"

"One thing about me that you might not know is that I'm a great multitasker." She smiles. "I can do two things at once."

I hum.

"What did you make?" she asks.

"It's just pasta and sauce. Both from a box or a can, so don't have super high expectations."

"Is there a way without using a box or a can?"

I slow blink. "Yes. You can make both from scratch."

She gapes. "You're telling me you know how to make pasta and sauce from scratch?"

"It's really not that hard."

"Why, Mr. Castelli. Aren't you just a surprise?"

I ignore her and take out two plates.

"Sorry for falling asleep earlier," she says. "I was waiting for you to come back because I didn't want to interrupt your call. The next thing I know, I wake up to the smell of oregano ... or whatever it is."

"I'm glad you got some rest. You needed it."

"Have you heard from Ford?"

I fix our plates, grabbing a piece of garlic bread for each of us, before sitting next to her at the counter. She hops up and grabs two bottles of water from the refrigerator.

"He called a little while ago," I say, watching her move gracefully through the kitchen. "He said they're sorting through things, and he'll let us know when he knows more."

I consider telling her what they found in her house and car but decide against it. We don't have any answers right now, and without a resolution, it might only make things worse for her. If I can't do anything else, I can shoulder the information on her behalf.

She hands me a bottle. "We might be here a while, huh?"

"Maybe."

She nods thoughtfully. "Then I want to say something to you."

"Shoot."

"About earlier, in the closet ..."

Her eyes are clear and alert. Her features are smooth and calm. She doesn't look perturbed or regretful, nor does she look upset with me. All good things.

"Dahlia, let me go first."

"Be my guest."

I take a breath and turn to face her. "That was on me. All of it. And I'm a prick for doing it. There are so many reasons it was wrong to almost kiss you that I wouldn't know where to start. Please accept my apology and know it won't happen again."

"Well, damn."

"Well, damn?"

She sighs, twirling her fork into her pasta. "You've complicated things."

"I know. I'm sorry."

"Not like that."

"Then how?"

She sets the fork down on the side of her plate, watching me out of the corner of her eye. I'm not sure what she's going to say. The woman's unreadable. But my heart pounds relentlessly, anyway, bracing for a turn in our relationship that I can't repair. I can't do anything to ruin that. I can't risk losing someone so important in my life. *I won't.*

"I was going to say that I didn't want it to make things weird between us," she says. "We've both had a wild day, and emotions got the best of us."

"You think?"

"Don't you?" She turns on the stool to face me head-on. "I was going to say that the moment in the closet was the realest thing I've felt in a long time. And it felt good, it was a relief, to finally pretend that's not what we want to do every time we're together."

What?

"I was pissed that you answered the phone, but I could've forgiven you," she says. "But now I know you think it was a giant mistake, so it's complicated."

"You can't possibly think crossing that line was smart."

She shrugs. "Why not?"

"Oh, I don't know. Should I count the ways?"

"How high do you need to count?" She watches me, unflinching. "We're both adults. We're trapped in a house together. We've been attracted to each other for a long damn time, and if you think this isn't going to come up when it's already come up and we've been in this house like five hours—and I've slept three of them—then you're a fool. And if you can't handle it, then call Theo and trade places."

Flames shoot out of the top of my head. "The fuck?"

"This has nothing to do with Theo. Not like that. And why do you care, anyway?"

I bite my tongue—afraid I'll say something I'll regret—even though the things I'd say are the truth.

She shrugs and goes back to her pasta. "Fine. We'll pretend you didn't just almost kiss me, and I didn't want it."

I get up from the table, Dahlia's words ringing through my mind.

"I was going to say that the moment in the closet was the realest thing I've felt in a long time."

That might be true for her. But that was the realest thing I've felt in my life.

"And it felt good, it was a relief, to finally pretend that's not what we want to do every time we're together."

And every time we're not.

It *was* a relief. Although we're handcuffed by our identities, for the briefest second in the closet, with her in my arms, I felt more freedom than I ever have in my life. It was as if the world stopped spinning, and nothing mattered but the two of us at that moment. The past was irrelevant. Questions about the future were immaterial. It didn't matter that we were co-workers, or that the risk of losing her or letting her down was unbearable. We just *were*.

I'll regret that we can't *be*—that I can't have *that, can't have her*—as long as I'm breathing.

Her fork scraping against the plate brings me back to the present. The weight of it all is unbearable.

I have to get out of this room. *Away from her.*

"I'm going to jump in the shower," I say.

"Fine."

"Fine."

I storm up the steps, pissed at myself ... and totally smitten with her.

I don't think this is what Ford meant when he told me to relax on this trip. It's yet another failure on my part.

Chapter Eleven

Dahlia

My chin rests on my knees.

The ocean sparkles, the waves gently lapping at the shore in the distance. From my perch tucked in the trees, the world is magical. Serene. Perfect.

If only that were true.

Troy didn't return, even after I'd finished dinner. I expected him to come back—I hoped he would. Sitting alone in a strange yet beautiful home, knowing that someone wants to kill me, makes me yearn for company.

I cleaned up his mess, loaded the dishwasher, and put the leftovers in the fridge. Then I found my way to a screened-in room on the third floor with the best views I've ever seen.

"What a waste," I whisper.

I can't video chat Morgan and show her this view. I can't even turn my phone on to snap a picture. My spirits sink as the weight of reality settles on my shoulders.

What will I do if this threat is real? What if it's not Freddy being a dumbass? Where will I go? What will I do? I can't sit here indefinitely because, let's face it, a white knight isn't coming.

He wouldn't even have dinner with me tonight.

I snort at the joke even though it wasn't funny.

"Hey." Troy appears in the doorway behind me, his hair still damp from his shower. "I couldn't find you."

"And you call yourself a professional."

He gives me a wobbly smile. "Want to go down to the beach?"

"I don't know. Are you going?"

"Well, you're not going alone."

I twist in my seat. "Since we just established that you're a shit bodyguard, would it really matter if I went alone?"

His smile fades. "I hope you're kidding."

"I think we've also already established that we don't always get what we hope for, haven't we?"

"Okay. You're pissed."

"No, Troy, I'm not pissed. *I'm tired.* I'm confused. I'm trying to have a good attitude about this whole nightmare, but the one person in the entire world who I can talk to just left me sitting by myself at dinner." I consider my words. "I guess I'm a little testy."

He runs a hand down his face and sighs. "I'm sorry. I should've stayed with you."

I start to razz him more, but the wariness in his eyes when he looks at me keeps me from it. Besides, I really don't want to bicker with him, whether I'm half joking or not.

"Fine," I say, getting up. "Let's go to the beach."

"Great," he mumbles, letting me lead the way.

We walk silently through the house, down the stairs, and onto the back patio. A loggia connects the house to a small building at the edge of the property. It sits beside a gate that opens to the sand.

The grounds behind the house are a storybook. Perfectly manicured landscaping, tiled walkways, and a fountain in the center of the yard create a relaxed atmosphere. Vines trail up the side of the buildings, and flowers bloom in a multitude of colors from the bushes dotting the space.

It's breathtaking.

We slip off our shoes at the gate. Troy pops a code into a keypad and then swings it open.

"Can you imagine living like this?" I ask, taking in our surroundings. I glance up and catch him watching me.

"Yeah. I can."

I'm not sure what he means—not with how he looks at me. So I tuck my chin and step onto the beach.

"Look at that sunset," I say as the sky transforms into a glorious array of colors. "My mom loved a pretty sunset."

"What was she like?"

"She was amazing. She was my best friend."

I smile as I think about her. It's almost strange to discuss her with Troy. Despite the attraction, we've always kept things fairly impersonal—*platonic*. We don't press too deeply into each other's lives and keep things superficial. But the question feels genuine, and surprisingly, sharing something so personal, so special to me, feels natural.

"I think about her every day. Some days are harder than others," I say, watching the sand squish between my toes. "She was a mother in every way—loving, protective, selfless. There was not a food she couldn't prepare, and she could turn a loaf of bread and a package of cheese into a meal fit for a king." I laugh. "She worked her ass off, working two jobs most of the time. But she didn't miss any of my sporting events or teacher conferences. And she didn't complain. She was proud ... maybe too proud."

Our feet sink into the wet sand as we walk along the water's edge. A peacefulness settles over me, soothing the raw edges of my nerves.

"How long were she and your dad together?" he asks.

"Not long." I gaze up at Troy. "My mother was working in a tailor's shop, and my dad brought a jacket to be hemmed. He says he fell in love with her at first sight. Her letter said he was the most handsome man she'd ever seen."

"Her letter?"

"Yeah." I kick a glob of sand, watching it land with a splat a few yards down the beach. "I never knew I had a father. She would say that my father loved me very much but had to go. She'd get emotional about it when I brought it up, so I didn't. I assumed he'd died."

Troy shoves his hands in his pockets. "How did you find out about him?"

"Well, it turns out that they were in contact all of my life."

"Are you serious?"

"Yeah." I shrug. "My dad's dad, so my grandfather, founded Dallo Metalworks. Apparently, he wasn't quite an upstanding citizen or a nice guy. When my mom found out she was pregnant, they panicked. Neither of them wanted me raised with anything to do with my grandfather. My dad said we still wouldn't be safe, even if he left with my mother and moved to the other side of the world."

"Your granddad was that bad?"

"That's what they say."

"So what happened? Your dad just walked away from you and your mom?"

I consider the question. It's not that easy.

"Kind of, I guess," I say. "Mom didn't want to abort me or put me up for adoption. And my dad didn't want her to do that either. So the only way they could guarantee that I wasn't in danger from one of my grandfather's schemes was for him to never know I existed. For *anyone* to know I existed."

His forehead pulls together. "So why did your dad come into your life now? If it's so dangerous, and it still is because we're here, why did he change course after all these years?"

"My grandfather died. I think I was thirteen or fourteen. My father inherited the company. It took him a few years to clean it up and make it more ... legitimate, I guess. By the time he was ready to figure out how to come into my life, my mom got sick."

"You'd think that was the perfect time to come into your life. He could've helped you cope."

"Maybe. Or he might have just inserted himself at a time when I needed to make as many memories with her as I could because her illness was terminal. Depends on how you look at it."

He nods his head, shuffling his feet through the water.

My heart hurts as I think of the pain my mom must've endured. Losing a man I believe she loved with all her heart—that's why she never dated or married. Dying young with a daughter barely in her twenties with no other family except a father she didn't know. She must've been terrified at the end and lonely in the middle.

I hate that for her. So much.

"But why *now*?" Troy asks.

I sigh. "When Mom was sick, and at the end of her life, she saw my dad. She asked him to see her, and he did. She wrote me a letter and gave it to him to give me if he ever thought the time was right to come into my life. The letter contained things that only she knew, and it was in her handwriting. It spelled out what happened between them and said that if Joseph Dallo handed me this letter, I could trust him. That she wanted me to." I smile sadly. "She told me once that a letter might appear one day written on her mother's rose stationery. And if it did, I should read it. I didn't know what that meant until my father handed me her letter."

"I'm just throwing this out there," he says carefully. "Do you find it ironic that he stayed out of your life because it wasn't safe for over twenty years, and when he decided to make contact with you, someone threatened your life?"

I can't deny it. That's *exactly* what it looks like. But my gut tells me it's not him, and I always trust my gut.

"It is ironic," I admit. "But I think it's a coincidence."

Troy sighs in frustration.

"What would he gain from threatening to kill me?" I ask. "I talk to him all the time. We have a solid relationship."

"You just met the guy."

"I just met you, and I trust you won't kill me. What's the difference?"

He stops himself from answering.

"It makes much more sense to me that it's Freddy," I say. "I don't know why no one believes that. He's angry with me. He's ... unhinged. He had access to my house because I'd given him a key."

Troy's lips form a tight line. "What's his motive?"

"I don't know. That he thought I'd get scared and run back to him? That if he can't have me, no one else will? He's not made sense for a while, which only backs up my point."

"When did he start not making sense?"

I think about it. "I'm not sure. Maybe ... six months ago?"

"What has he been weird about? How did his behavior change?"

"He became erratic. Paranoid. He started buying things he couldn't afford." I look at Troy over my shoulder. "But now I know he was doing cocaine, so that fits the narrative."

"You were never scared of him?"

I laugh. "Uh, no. I could probably take him in a fight. And, besides, I think he knew my dad would come for him if he hurt me."

"Freddy knows about your dad?"

"Yeah, a few people do. It was hard keeping it from him when we practically lived together when I found out." I think back to that time. "He didn't love the idea that Joseph Dallo was my father. He thought he was a rich prick who'd walk away from me again."

Troy hums. "Can I ask you something else?"

"Sure."

"I notice you never call Joseph *Dad*. You say *my dad* or *my father*. But never *Dad*."

"Yeah, I don't know why. I've let it slip a time or two, but it's just ... he didn't play catch with me in the yard. He didn't pick me up from school or tuck me in at night. I didn't grow up thinking he was the biggest, strongest man in the world. So maybe I want to preserve that title for someone who embodies it." I shrug. "I imagine hearing my children call my husband *Dad* someday, and it feels so special. I want it to feel special. It *should* feel special."

He considers this as we stop and look across the ocean. Birds dip into the water, looking for fish. A boat sails in the distance. I don't know if it's the salt in the air or if my defenses are whittled down, but sharing this with Troy allows me to breathe a little easier.

"What about your parents?" I ask, taking the focus off me. "What are they like?"

Troy's entire demeanor changes. His hands come out of his pockets. Shadows fall across his face. He looks at the ground as we walk, his lips pressed into a thin line.

"I'm sorry," I say. "We don't have to talk about them."

He forces a swallow and heaves a breath. Finally, he speaks. "Parent is such a loaded word."

I nod but stay quiet.

"Let's just say that my parents were the opposite of yours," he says. "They weren't in love. They didn't stick to their word. And they sure as hell didn't sacrifice anything for Travis and me."

My heart twists in my chest at the emotion—an angry, painful, resolved display visible on Troy's face. I want to hug him, wrap my arms around his waist, and wipe the loneliness away from his features. But he's already told me that's not going to happen. And he's probably right.

So I don't.

"I'm sorry you experienced that," I say softly.

"It made me who I am, I guess."

"Well, if it matters at all, I think you're a pretty great guy. You're highly annoying a lot of the time, and you can be *so* demanding and bossy." I wink at him. "But you're a good man."

His pace slows as he watches me.

"What?" I ask, laughing. "Why are you looking at me like that?"

Slowly, a smile inches across his cheeks. "I'm not looking at you like anything."

"Yes, you are."

He chuckles. "I don't think anyone has ever told me that before."

"No one has told you what?"

He stops with his back to the horizon. The golden hour beautifully illuminates his features, and the wind pulls his shirt tight against his body. As attractive as the image is, my favorite part of the picture is not his muscles, shoulders, or chiseled jawline.

It's his eyes.

The gray is light, almost blue, and they're lit in a way I've never noticed before. Coupled with the soft, almost shy smile he bestows upon me, I'm speechless.

"No one has ever told me I'm a good man," he says.

"Seriously?"

He shrugs as if he's embarrassed.

"Troy ..." I flinch, finding it hard to believe. "No one has ever told you that? Ever?"

"Never. It's stupid, and I shouldn't have said anything because now you're looking at me like—"

"*Hey.*"

He stops, startled by my interruption.

My heart tugs in my chest. It's obviously such a painful point for him. *Can he possibly not know how wonderful he is?* I'm unsure how this ties into his childhood, but I'm certain it does.

I want to hug him so damn bad, but I'm afraid he'll pull away.

If he needs the reassurance that he's not like his parents, I'm happy to give it to him. But I'll have to give it to him in a way that he won't shut right down.

I ponder my words carefully.

"I don't want to inflate your ego or anything, and this actually hurts *my* ego a bit because I'm about to tell you how great you are, and you refused to kiss me ..."

He bites his lip, warning me not to go there.

"You are ... really amazing, actually," I say.

His lip pops free.

"You're intelligent and loyal. Probably the most loyal person I know," I say, my voice carrying away on the breeze. "You're a good friend. You're honest and kind. You're brave. You're selfless ... most of the time."

He chuckles, his cheeks turning a shade of pink.

"I mean, look at you right now," I say. "You just shelved your entire life and came here to protect a woman you work with because her asshole ex-boyfriend is fucking with her. That's not mediocre-man stuff, Troy. That's not even lukewarm-man stuff. That's great-man stuff, and if no one has ever told you that, then let me be the first."

The water laps at our ankles, pulling the sand out from around our feet as it recedes. The breeze licks at the edges of our clothes and the ends of my hair. It's as if Troy and I are in a cocoon, insulated from the outside world. Safe from all harm—physically and emotionally.

"You almost had that right," he says.

"What do you mean?"

"I shelved my entire life and came here to protect a woman." He closes the distance between us. "But she's not just a woman I work with."

My heart skips a beat as I stare into his eyes. "Is that so?"

"She's brilliant and hard-working and one of the sweetest people I've ever met even though she somehow weaponizes that sometimes."

I try not to giggle.

"She's a bit of a pain in the ass, but I find myself looking forward to dealing with her every day," he says, smiling softly. "She's strong and fearless ... and wildly, ridiculously beautiful."

I gasp, holding my breath.

"If she wasn't my co-worker, and I wasn't on duty, and I wasn't so fucked up that it would undoubtedly ruin everything between us eventually, I'd shoot my shot and pray that it works."

As soon as the words leave his mouth, his features harden. It's as if he said too much, let his guard down too low, and is preparing for a pushback.

Nope. Sorry, Troy. You don't get to take that back.

I turn toward the house. "Well, it's a good thing she's your co-worker, and you're on duty because if your shot looks anything like it did in the closet this afternoon, it needs some work."

His gaze snaps to mine, bewildered.

I laugh. "Let's get back. I need a shower."

Relief washes across his face, so I wink at him.

"Too bad you have such a shit game," I say, walking backward so I can see him. "Or you could've joined me in that shower."

My laughter trails me as I jog back to the house.

"She's strong and fearless ... and wildly, ridiculously beautiful."

I'm not sure what just happened, but I know he'll need time to process that.

And maybe, so will I.

Chapter Twelve

Dahlia

I scrunch the ends of my wet hair with a towel and look at myself in the foggy bathroom mirror. My cheeks are rosy, and despite my earlier nap, there are bags beneath my eyes. But, by far, the worst part of the image looking back at me is my hair. I rack my brain, trying to remember what I shoved in my bag last night before I left for Morgan's. I know I packed a detangling comb. It must've fallen out of my cosmetics bag inside my backpack.

How was that just last night?

I take a step back and look at my reflection again.

Troy's shirt, a soft black fabric that smells faintly of his cologne, hits me mid-thigh. My clothes from Morgan's were soaked, thanks to a smashed water bottle buried in my stuff. Luckily, there was a stack of Troy's clean T-shirts on the bathroom counter. Figuring he wouldn't mind, I helped myself to one.

The feeling of his shirt against my naked skin is more erotic than it should be. Every time the material brushes against my nipples or swishes against my ass cheeks, a rush of energy shoots through me as if Troy was touching me himself.

A girl can freaking wish.

I dry my hair again and head into the bedroom to search for my comb. I come to a screeching halt when Troy appears in the doorway to the hall. Black sweatpants, no shirt—the man is a whole damn meal.

I'm not sure I'm strong enough for this.

He looks me up and down, taking his time as he gazes at the length of my body. I don't mind. It affords me a moment to drink him in, too.

"Nice shirt," he says, lifting his eyes from my tits to my face.

"Didn't think you'd mind. *Hope you don't mind.* It was this or I was going naked. All my clothes are soaked from an exploded water bottle."

He rolls a suitcase into the room and places it by the closet. "Your stuff came. Grey dropped it off a little while ago."

"Should we unpack or just assume this might be over tomorrow?"

Troy frowns. "I don't think it'll be over that fast. Stay positive but base it in reality."

"Have you heard anything?"

"They're tracing the IP address from the email and looking at security footage from your neighborhood. Ford has someone tailing Freddy, too." His brows pull together. "What kind of name is that, anyway? *Freddy.* Did his mother hate him?"

I grin. "I hope whoever's tailing him likes strip clubs because that's where he spent the past couple of weeks of our relationship." *Or likely through our relationship, but I don't really give a damn now.*

"Did you know my first job at Landry Security, once I left Barrett's team, was at a strip club?"

I laugh. "Are you serious?"

"Yeah. These two football players, Best and Miller from the Legends, came to town. They just won the big game and were in town to party with someone. Can't remember who. Anyway, Sebastian and I were assigned to them for the weekend, and I saw more asses shaking, tits bouncing, and bills flying than I've ever seen for a continued stretch of time in my life."

"I'm jealous. Not of the strip club, per se," I say, adding the last bit in quickly. "But you guys have such exciting jobs. Office work isn't fun."

"But you have Snack Wednesdays."

"Shut up." I laugh, sitting on the edge of the bed. "I want to go into the field and work, even if it's only for one job."

"Not happening."

"Love the opinion, but let's remember you aren't my boss."

He lifts a brow. "Sure."

"Don't patronize me. You know I could talk Ford into letting me try it."

"Until I threaten to quit. Then your cute little ass will be back behind your desk."

I gasp.

He shakes his head. "Look, I don't mean that like it sounds. I'm not one of those assholes that thinks a woman should be in the office or the kitchen. That's bullshit. But I do think you, specifically, aren't equipped to deal with shooters, home invasions, and men with knives. Do a few years of training and then come talk to me."

I smile.

"But you're still not going out there."

"Troy!" I laugh again, pulling the blankets down. "Have you felt this mattress yet? It's a freaking cloud."

He presses his palms on the bed. "You shouldn't have a hard time sleeping in here."

"What about you?"

"I'll take the couch."

"Oh. Okay."

I turn away from him, so he won't see the disappointment on my face. It's not like I expected him to fuck me or anything, but I did hope I wouldn't be alone. I've kept it together all day, and I'm proud of myself for that. *But the night?* Nights hit differently after a good day. This has not generally been one of those.

"Are we stuck in this house the whole time we're here?" I ask, slipping under the blankets and getting comfortable on the pillows.

"Got somewhere you want to go?"

I shrug. "I don't know. I flipped through this booklet about the island while you took your marathon shower to avoid me earlier, and there's this charming little village with a coffee shop and a bookstore not too far from here. I thought maybe we could explore it one day."

He's clearly bothered by this but doesn't want an argument. "Maybe. Let's see what happens."

Good enough. "What do you usually do at night?"

"Depends where I am."

"Right. Okay. What if you're home?"

He drops to the floor and begins pumping out push-ups. I peer over the end of the bed to watch. His back muscles ripple with each movement, and I wonder why someone hasn't videotaped this and sold it online as porn. Because this little show makes me as wet as anything.

Damn.

"What are you doing?" I ask, laughing.

"I didn't get a workout in today."

I snort. "I think you'll be just fine missing one workout."

He pushes his body up and down with what looks like very little effort.

"What if you're home?" I ask again.

"If I'm home, I change clothes. I like to work out before I eat if I can help it. Grab a shower. Then I sit in the living room or bed and read a book or watch television."

"What do you read?"

He groans, breathing harder as he bangs out a few more push-ups. Then he rocks back and sits on his knees. "What do I read?" He shrugs. "It depends. I like biographies. Fiction. I also really like those coffee table books on specific topics."

"You're so surprising."

"What?" He smiles. "Did you think I didn't read?"

"No. It's just when I think you couldn't possibly get any hotter, you find a way to throw more gas on the fire."

His smile turns mischievous. "I'm hot, huh?"

"I think we're beyond pretending like we aren't attracted to each other."

"Fair enough. What do you do at night?"

My cheeks flame, and I can't wipe the smile off my face.

"What?" he asks, grinning. "Tell me."

I try to answer him with a response that leaves out masturbating while imagining him doing dirty things to me as the last thing I do. But the amusement on his face, like he suspects the truth, keeps me from speaking.

"Doll ..."

I wiggle deeper under the blankets. "I go to yoga or Pilates. Go home. Eat with Burt half the time."

"Burt?"

"My neighbor. He's in his midseventies, and we're *best neighbors*, he says. He doesn't have kids and isn't married, and I feel bad for the guy. I don't think he has a lot of extra cash, so I bring enough dinner home or cook enough for both of us most nights."

Troy gets to his feet and stretches. "That's really nice of you."

"I don't do it for an *atta girl*."

"I didn't say you did. But it's still nice of you." He sits on the edge of the bed. "What do you do after you eat?"

"Shower. Get my picture taken, apparently."

His eyes darken.

"Then watch a cooking show or read a romance novel. Sometimes, I pretend I'm going to meal prep, and I make these specific menus that look amazing on paper. I've never once used them."

He laughs.

"That's it. I'm incredibly boring," I say.

"Tell me more about your romance novels. Are they filthy? Pure smut? What kind of things are you into?"

My throat tightens as a flame is lit to my libido. Troy in sweats and no shirt is one thing. Troy in sweats, no shirt—sans push-ups—and wanting me to discuss smut is a whole different animal.

"It's a little of everything," I say, watching his reactions closely. I squeeze my thighs to help quell the ache building there. "Sometimes I go for the sweet, small-town boys. Other times, I'm into the billionaire bad boys." I smirk. "I have moments where I want erotica and read it just for the sex."

"I see." He shifts his weight on the bed. "What's the hottest thing you've ever read?"

"Ever?"

"Ever."

I laugh. "There's no way to pick just one. They're all so different." I hold his gaze. "Now, if you're asking me what I think is hot in real life, that's a different story."

"That's what I'm asking."

His tone is low and gravelly, scraping over my flesh. I shiver beneath the blankets and wonder how far I can push this conversation ... and if I should. He's the one who put the brakes on earlier. He's made it clear that we need boundaries—and he's not wrong. But this feels so natural. *It feels so damn good.* He has to know he's throwing fuel on the fire.

I glance at him and find him smirking.

Fine. I'll toss a match on your gasoline.

"I don't mind a little choking," I say, smirking back at him. "A little spanking. I think it's hot when the guy lets you know what they enjoy so you can please them and then have him tell you how good you are."

Troy's eyes blaze. He balls the blankets in his hands, squeezing them until his knuckles turn white.

"Now let me ask you something," I say. "What's the difference between this conversation and kissing me? I'm curious."

"This is just a conversation. But if I kiss you, that's different. I'll want to do it again. And you might get the impression that I'm the kind of guy that a girl like you could have a real relationship with. That assumption will cause problems."

"Because you're not that kind of guy?"

"No. I'm not."

"Why?"

He falls onto his back and looks at the ceiling. "I'm fucked up."

"Aren't we all?"

"I mean it."

"So let's say you're right. You're fucked up. Does that make you unqualified to be happy?"

He doesn't answer me.

"We're all fucked up in one way or the other, Troy."

"I'm thirty-seven. You're twenty ... six?"

"Close enough."

He sighs, rolling onto his side to face me. "You have your whole life ahead of you. You can get married. Have kids. Be the mother that your mother was to you."

"And you can't do those things?"

"No."

His answer is without hesitation—straightforward and simple. It hurts my heart. *Why does he think he's bound to be alone?*

"I think you sell yourself short," I say.

"I think you don't really know me."

"I think that might be true. It's sad that I have to trust you with my life, and you can't trust me enough to let me know who you really are."

Silence falls in the room.

I move my leg away from him. "What do you think, hypothetically speaking because I'm not trying to kiss you right now, would happen if we kissed? I'm just curious about your thought process because it provides a little insight into your psyche." I narrow my eyes, thinking. "Are you trying to convince me you're unworthy so I won't want to get to know you?"

"Maybe."

"Well, first, I don't believe that for a second. Second, you should know me better by now. The entire world thinks my dad is a piece of shit, and until he shows me that himself, I believe he's not. I believe in giving people the benefit of the doubt. And if you think that I won't give you, of all people, that grace, then you're ridiculous."

"It's not that simple."

"Maybe not. But it's a damn shame that you live your life alone when you have so much to offer someone."

He studies me, and I let him. Maybe he'll see I'm telling the truth.

Not that it matters. This conversation is more about me not thinking about people wanting to kill me than it is anything else. It's a distraction. But I do wish that Troy would listen to me. I won't hold my breath.

I yawn and snuggle into my pillows. He gets up and turns off the light.

"I'll let you get some sleep," he says.

But as soon as I'm about to close my eyes, my heart pounds. *Hard.* Shadows dance across the walls, and a cold sweat coats my back.

Suddenly, I remember every word of that email.

Run or die.

Don't alert the authorities, or I'll make the choice for you.

I can't stop thinking about someone being in my house. About the nuance of those terrifying images of me out living my life while being watched. *How long have they been watching me? How did I never notice?*

They were in my bedroom ... could they be in here, too?

I know it's not likely. It may even be impossible. But it's all raw and fresh in my mind and still very real, and I don't want to be alone.

"Troy?" I ask, my voice wavering.

"Yeah?"

I take a deep breath, thankful for the shroud of darkness. "I'm not as brave as you think I am."

He moves silently across the room and climbs into bed next to me. He doesn't touch me or even come too close.

I smile all the same. "Thank you."

My eyelids get heavy, and my breathing slows. Sleep welcomes me into its peacefulness, and I know it's because of Troy's presence. His warmth. His protection.

I'm safe with him.

"Dahlia?"

"Yeah?" I ask sleepily.

"I'm not as brave as you think I am either."

Before I can answer him, I drift off into a land of dreams.

Chapter Thirteen

T roy

Boom.

A crack of thunder shakes the house, coaxing me from a deep sleep.

Rain hammers the windows in a relentless assault as bolts of lightning streak the dark sky. The wind whips outside, bending the palm trees at unnatural angles. It's a dreary, ominous morning. The only positive is the woman lying beside me.

Dahlia's strawberry-hued hair is spread across the white pillowcase, her lips pressed together in a sweet pout. I woke up at dawn and watched her sleep for an hour. She's so peaceful, *so fucking beautiful*, that it's hard to comprehend.

How is she real? How is she here, in this bed, with me?

I lie quietly and mull over yesterday. I wait for a moment of panic to rip through me. But it doesn't come.

By all indications, I should be extricating myself from this situation. My ass should be on the phone with Ford, requesting someone take my place because the majority of yesterday afternoon was highly inappropriate and unprofessional. I have never, not once, even considered getting involved with someone I was hired to protect.

Never.

I didn't consider getting involved with Dahlia either. *Have I thought about it?* A million times. *Have I wished it could happen?* Every day since I met her. But I know that can't happen. I know I'd ruin her—taint her world with a stain she doesn't need. *So why in the hell did things get so out of control? Why did I ask her questions about her sexual preferences, for fuck's sake?*

And why am I still in bed with her?

I study the curve of her lips and the bend of her neck. Her jawline is soft and smooth. Her lashes are dark and long. She's the epitome of beauty in every way, and being near her, interacting with her, and sharing her space makes me feel something strange.

It's a way I've never felt before.

It's a way that, if things were different, I could get used to.

"*Ah.*"

Her lips part, and a soft moan slips through the room. The sound, sweet and sexy, sends a shot straight to my cock.

"*Oh.*" She lifts her chin, the corner of her eyes creasing. "*There.*"

The word is mumbled but discernible.

She moans again, squirming beneath the blankets. My heart hammers in my chest. My balls tighten so hard it hurts.

The edge of her shirt—*my shirt*—rides up her side. She kicks the blankets until they sit just above her hip and expose her bare skin from below her navel to just below her tits.

Every cell in my body is on high alert as I watch her hand slide between her legs.

This can't be happening.

I shouldn't be here. I shouldn't be watching this ... but I'll be damned if I get up.

She sucks a breath in through her teeth, arching her back off the bed. Her knees spread. The blanket dips again, lower this time, until her pussy is barely covered.

My God.

I fold my hands on my chest, refusing to let them go anywhere near my cock. I grit my teeth and watch her hand move against her clit just inches from me.

It's torture—complete, absolute fucking torture.

Dahlia hisses, sliding a hand up her shirt. The material lifts and sits on her chest, exposing her tight nipple and round, heavy breast. She palms herself, rolling her nipple between two manicured fingers.

I blow out a breath slowly, trying desperately not to touch her. But fucking hell, it's hard—in every way.

"*Troy,*" she whispers on a moan, her legs falling farther apart.

My teeth grind together, my eyes glued to her mouth.

I can't do this. Should I do this? Do I need to get up?

Will it wake her if I do?

I don't want to embarrass her—and there's nothing to be embarrassed about. I'd pay for this experience.

I lift my head off the pillow, planning on slipping out of the room and jacking off in the shower. But as I move, she moves. And as she moves, the blankets move. And as the cool air touches her damp flesh, her eyes open ... and gaze straight into mine.

Her pupils widen as she realizes what's happening. Panic begins to set in.

"Don't," I whisper.

"What was ... what's happening?" She looks down, watching as her hand slips from between her legs. "*Oh my God.*"

She grabs the edge of the blanket and pulls it over her body.

My brain is a cacophony of thoughts. The one side reminds me this is inappropriate and probably against work protocol in several ways. The other voice points out that we're already here, it's going to be even more awkward if I just get up ... and that we both want to fuck.

There are a million reasons that's a bad idea, but as she looks at me—begging me to fix this situation, I can't remember one of them.

I pull the blanket off myself, showing her my dick stretching against the fabric of my sweatpants.

"*Oh*," she says, her lips parting.

I gulp, waiting for her to fully awaken. If this goes anywhere, I need to know she made the choice coherently.

I need to know she wanted it ... that she wants me.

"I didn't touch you," I say softly. "I wouldn't do that."

She licks her lips. "I know you didn't."

"How?"

She brings her eyes to mine. "I didn't come."

Her words ignite a firestorm inside me, and I suddenly don't give a damn about whatever reasons I had not to touch her.

I want her.

I need her.

I have to have her ... *now*.

"Do you want to come?" I ask, my heart striking my ribs with every beat.

"Are you offering to help?" She pulls the blankets off so hard they fall off the side of the bed. "Or do you wanna watch?"

Fuck.

Dahlia rolls onto her back, bending her knees and letting them fall to the side—giving me full view of her pussy. She holds my gaze as her fingers drag between her tits, over her stomach, and between her thighs. Her eyes flutter closed as she whimpers.

It takes everything I have not to pull her beneath me and sink into her as far as I can go.

But I don't. Even though I can't recall why I'm not supposed to do this, I know that if I do, things won't be the same.

If I touch her, *she's mine*.

There will be no going back.

"Are you sure?" I ask, my voice rough.

She giggles, fluttering her lashes at me. "I couldn't be surer."

"I'm serious. This is going to complicate things between us infinitely."

"Troy, if you haven't noticed, things are infinitely more complicated between us now, whether I come on my fingers or on your cock."

I shudder at the energy centering in my groin. My stomach's clenched so tight that I grimace.

"I don't have any condoms," I say.

Her jaw hangs open, and her hand pulls away from her clit. It rests on her stomach. Wetness coats her fingers, and I force myself to look away.

"*How?*" she asks. "How do you not have a condom?"

I chuckle at the look on her face. "This was a work trip."

"And you don't always carry some around with you?"

"No, I don't," I say, my chuckle becoming a laugh. "I don't normally fuck on the clock."

She grins. "That's good to know."

"This is your call."

"I went to the doctor when I broke up with Freddy to ensure things were good. All clear. I prioritize my birth control appointments. I assure you I'm ninety-whatever percent unable to get pregnant today."

The thought of impregnating her turns me on.

What the fuck?

"What about you?" she asks.

"They ran every panel available on me when that guy sliced me with a knife at Laina's concert a couple of months ago. I haven't had sex since."

Her lips break into a wide smile, her eyes twinkling with mischief.

"Then you have two choices, Mr. Castelli."

I grin. "Give them to me."

She sits up with her legs tucked under her. Her hair brushes against her shoulders in wild waves. The way her tits hang, the soft curve of her stomach, the bend of her hips—she's an irresistible picture that's burned into my mind.

A picture of perfection.

"Option one," she says, smirking. "Fuck me."

I groan, holding myself back. "And two?"

"Get off the damn bed."

Chapter Fourteen

Dahlia

Troy's lips twist, and for a split second, I worry he'll mess with me or, even worse, start talking logic and nonsense.

I don't have time for that today. I don't want to hear it.

Our chemistry is going to explode sooner or later. It's futile to deny it. It might as well be a controlled burn before it blows up in our faces. *Not to mention—I'm horny as hell.*

I gather my hair into a ponytail, hoping he answers quickly. I'm about to combust.

He lifts up and slips off his sweatpants.

"*Come here,*" he says, reaching for me.

I lay my palm in his and straddle him. I'm so wet I slide along his rock-hard shaft, hissing at the pressure against my throbbing clit. I want him inside me so bad.

"You're a fucking vision," he says, gripping my hips.

I run my hands across his shoulders and down his chest, committing every peak and valley of his muscles to memory.

He grins. "I don't know what to do."

I laugh at the bewildered look on his face. "That's not what I thought you were going to say. But you're lucky because I ..." I grind on top of his dick. "*Do.*"

"Do I savor this moment? Or do I fuck the hell out of you?"

"That's quite a conundrum. But I think I have a solution."

He lifts his brows.

"Fuck me now," I say, bringing his hands to my chest. He cups my breasts, holding their weight in his palms. "Savor me later."

Troy rolls my nipples between his fingers. "This might ruin our working relationship."

I hum as my eyes flutter closed. He thrusts against my soaked flesh, sending a wave of pleasure through me.

"You'll be mine after this," he says.

I look at him and smile, my heart filling with affection for this beautifully broken, *good man.*

"I'm pretty sure I'm already yours. It's just that neither of us have admitted it yet."

His sweet, soft grin is one I haven't seen before. It's one I'd do anything to see again. And to know that I'm the one who put it there —that he trusts me enough to show me—means the world.

He cups the sides of my face and lowers me to him.

And I melt.

His soft lips move slowly against mine, sending a shiver through my body. His tongue slides past my lips and sweeps lazily through my mouth.

He pulls away, brushing my hair away from my face.

"I've wanted to do that for a long time," he says, peering up at me. "Now, are you ready to get fucked?"

A crack of thunder snaps through the air, followed by a streak of lightning that lights up the room.

"Yes," I pant. "*Please.*"

He lifts me and grabs his cock. "I like a woman with manners."

The tip parts my folds and dips into my wetness. I hover above it, holding my breath, feeling the anticipation reach a frenzied crescendo.

My thighs are sticky. Sweat coats my skin. I can feel the heat of my pussy as it begs to be opened and filled with his cock.

Thunder ricochets through the air as Troy's fingertips dig into my waist. It's not a gentle grip—*it burns*.

Our gazes collide. Troy's eyes are as wild as mine. A coy smile dusts his lips.

"Ride this dick." He guides me down, filling my pussy as I take him deep inside me. "*Just like that.* Do you feel yourself getting stretched?"

"*Fuck, yes.*" I blow out a shaky breath, ending it with a laugh. "I'm afraid to move. I might come already."

"This shall be a lesson in restraint for both of us then because you feel so good, so tight, *so wet* that I could blow inside you right now."

The desire in his eyes ratchets up my need for him another notch. To know this man wants me this badly is the biggest turn-on—*ever*.

I start to ride him, working a slow, methodical circle on his cock. He hisses a breath, groaning as I shift in the other direction.

"*My God,*" he says, palming my tits.

I grin, adding a little lift to the motion. "I take it that you like this."

He hums, rubbing my pebbled nipples with his thumbs.

"You feel so good inside me, Troy," I say, grinding on him. I lean back, gripping his legs to hold me up, and continue to move. "I can feel the ridges of your cock and the swollen head. It's fucking amazing."

He rubs my clit with just the right amount of pressure, gripping my ass with his other hand. Each movement sends a burst of flames through my core. Each flame brings me closer to the orgasm that's just beyond my reach.

"I want to watch you come just like this," he says. "I want to watch your pussy pulse and those fucking tits bounce. I want to watch your face as you fall apart for me."

"Well, keep doing that," I groan, "and you'll get your wish."

"I've already gotten my wish, Doll. This is just a bonus."

I can't take it.

"You're starting to shake," he says, increasing the pressure on my sensitive bud. "Are you going to come for me?"

"*Yes.*"

The first waves lick at my core, warning me of the tsunami about to hit. I hesitate, whimpering as I prepare myself for what's to come.

"Don't stop," he says, lifting his hips into me. "Ride this all the way out."

The buildup comes fast and strong. The orgasm crashes over me, sending wave after wave of pleasure flooding my body.

"God, you're beautiful," Troy says as if he's in awe.

I cry out as the climax hits, yelling his name so loud that it echoes through the house.

"There you go," he says, holding me down against him and fucking me from below. "Does that feel good?"

"Yes," I say through clenched teeth. "It's so good. So ... *fucking good.*"

I whine as the sensation slows, and I drift back to earth. My thighs burn. My arms shake, nearly giving out. I struggle to sit up again with Troy still rock hard inside me.

His smirk is decadent. "How do you feel?"

I do a quick assessment. But instead of feeling the burn in my thighs and the weakness in my arms, I feel a flicker of desire deep in my belly.

I lean forward and press a kiss to the center of his lips. He threads his fingers through my hair and holds me in place.

The kiss is smooth, decadent, and totally unrushed. It starkly contrasts with the flurry and power of the previous moments.

He breaks the kiss. I lean back and then climb off him.

"*Oof,*" I groan, my pussy aching. Before I can get my wits about me, Troy grabs my ankles and drags me to the edge of the bed.

His eyes are dark, maybe even a little dangerous in the sexiest, most carnal way. The small bloom of desire blossoms into full-blown *need*.

The sweetness of his kiss and the consideration of the first round are nowhere to be seen. This Troy is different. This Troy is about to fuck me hard. *And I am absolutely here for it.*

"Get on your hands and knees," he says.

My insides quiver as I do as I'm told.

"Look at this ass," he says, spreading my cheeks with his hands.

I laugh. "Nothing's going in this ass. Let's be clear."

He strikes his hand against the center of one cheek, and the smack rings through the room.

My eyes open wide as the sting bites through my core, leaving me wanting more.

His thumb presses against my puckered hole.

"Troy," I say, my body clenching. "Don't."

"I won't. Yet."

"Or ever."

"We'll see."

I laugh, but the sound is stolen by a moan as his finger slides through my slit. "*Fuck.*"

"One of these days, I'm going to taste you," he says, inserting one, then two fingers inside me. "I'm going to bury my tongue in this sweet little cunt and make you come all over my face."

I tremble, my breath shaking as it releases from my lungs.

"But right now, I want to bury myself inside you," he says, massaging my ass with one hand. "I want to feel you clenching around me. I want to know how deep I can go."

"Let's do it."

He chuckles, popping his palm against my backside again. This time, I yelp. He immediately rubs the spot and then presses a kiss against it.

My arms go weak. My head dangles between them. I don't know if it's the belated effect of the orgasm, the anticipation of what's to come, or the adrenaline that makes me so wobbly.

He grips my hips and presses against my pussy. Before I can prepare myself, he thrusts into me without mercy.

"Dammit," I yell, my eyes bulging.

"You said you wanted fucked."

"*Ah!*"

He slams into me so hard that I nearly fall face-first into the mattress. Each stroke is a tease—the satisfaction of being filled by his cock, followed by the anticipation of it returning. Over and over and over.

This is my favorite form of fucking—being pounded so deeply that there's no room to think about anything else.

"Is this what you wanted?" he asks, gripping me so hard I wince.

"*Yes.*"

"Can you feel my cock throbbing? That's just for you. God, *you make me so fucking hard.*" He growls, the sound prickling my skin. "Arch your back for me, Doll."

I squeeze my eyes shut, tears gathering in the corners from the intensity. "Fuck me harder."

He chuckles, grabbing my ponytail and wrapping it around his hand. Then he tugs my head backward.

My scalp *stings.* My pussy *throbs.* My thoughts are gloriously suspended, only able to focus on the pleasure overtaking my body.

"You are so fucking perfect," he says. "I love how you take this dick."

I whimper as I arch my back for him, causing my ass to lift—and allowing Troy to bury himself even deeper.

"Just like that," I say, barely able to get the words out of my parched throat. I lick my lips. "*Oh my God.*"

"Tell me what you want," he says, grinding his cock into me. "Have you had enough? Or do you want more?"

I'm clinging to reality, dangling on the precipice of another orgasm. This one, I already know, will be all I can handle.

"Come in me," I say as he yanks on my ponytail again. "I want to

Pulse

feel you blow as deep as you can get. Let me feel how much you want me."

"*Fucking hell.*"

He lets go of my hair and grips my waist again. It takes no time for him to find a rhythm and less time for my orgasm to find me.

I close my eyes, panting in anticipation of the surge rising from my core. It's a wave coming in hot—and there's no stopping it. There's no controlling it. There's nothing I can do but let it ravage me.

"I'm going to come," I say, my body beginning to quicken.

He cracks my ass sharply—and that does it. *That's what I needed.*

"*Troy!*" I scream as I fall apart.

My elbows bend, and my shoulders fall toward the mattress. My sight is cut off by a burst of glittered colors that drift through the air.

He holds me up, bouncing me off his cock before he finally buries himself to the hilt.

"*Fuck,*" he groans, his body shaking behind me. He pulls out and then slowly slides back in. "*Motherfucker.*"

My pussy is on fire, squeezing his cock, milking it for every last drop of cum.

"That feels *so good,*" I say, my head spinning. It feels so amazing, I want to cry.

He sags against me for a moment, rubbing his hand tenderly across my ass.

"Are you okay?" he asks softly.

"You could say that."

He pulls out of me much easier than he went into me and guides me to the mattress.

I lie on my stomach with my cheek pressed against the mattress. I'm unsure if I could pick my head up if I wanted to.

He lies beside me and brushes my hair out of my face.

"You never stop amazing me," he says, grinning. "I want to make sure you're okay."

"Do I look okay?" I ask, the words muffled by the bed.

He chuckles. "You look gorgeous, but that wasn't the question."

125

I suck up the spit in my mouth and lift my head. "Yes. I'm actually really fucking great right now although it might take me a minute to find the use of my legs."

"How about this. I'll fill the tub with a bubble bath. When it's ready, I'll carry you to it."

My heart swells.

This is the Troy I suspected was buried under those layers of grumpiness. He's a sweet, kind man who isn't quite as hard as he makes himself out to be. But that's okay. I know he's there. And as long as he feels safe enough with me to be this way, that's all that matters.

"Only if you'll get in with me." I smile at him.

His face lights up. "Deal."

Who said you can't have dessert at the beginning of the day? If I'm lucky, I might get an afternoon snack, too.

Chapter Fifteen

Dahlia

"Is this everything you thought it would be?" Troy asks, splashing warm water gently onto my chest.

He sits behind me in the tub, his front to my back, and holds me like we've done this a hundred times.

I lean my head on his chest and poke my toes out of the bubbles, thinking about my mom's thoughts on baths being the epitome of sophistication. This is decadent, but more because of the man holding me and less about the bathtub.

"No," I say.

"No?"

"No. It's not everything I thought it would be."

"Why? I want this to meet your expectations. I can't fail you now."

I laugh. "When I dreamed of this bathtub experience, it didn't have a gorgeous man who has a bit of an attitude problem from time to time but can also be pretty damn sweet when he wants to be, sitting with his arms around me." I tilt my head back so I can see his face. "This is so much better than I thought it would be."

He presses a kiss to my forehead, and I all but swoon.

We've sat here for a long time—long enough for the hot water to cool twice. Troy ran downstairs during the second refill and got us water and a bag of Doritos that he found in the pantry.

The bathroom is humid. Steam fogs the vanity mirrors. It's cozy and warm ... and wonderful.

"This is a new experience for me, you know," I say, drawing circles onto Troy's muscled forearms.

"What? Taking a bath with someone?"

"Um, no. I've done that."

He bristles. "Let's move this conversation along."

I laugh again, my damp hair sticking to his chest. "I don't normally feel this relaxed around someone. I usually make them work for it."

"You don't think I worked for it?"

"No."

"*Okay.* Do you have any idea how hard it has been to work with you every motherfucking day for the past two years and try to pretend you're just another girl?"

I scoff. "That's not working for it. That's working *not* for it or something."

"That doesn't even make sense."

"Yes, it does," I say. "You were actively working on *not* hooking up with me. That's not working *for it,* Castelli."

His chest rises and falls, moving me with it.

"I want to be clear about something," he says, his tone somber.

"What?"

"This wasn't a hookup."

My chest fills with a warmth that's so unexpected that I squirm.

"I warned you. I—"

"Oh, I remember. I wanted fucked, and you wanted to have a

conversation about condoms, and work complications, and sexually transmitted diseases, and—"

"It's called being responsible."

I look back at him and smile. "I know. Honestly, I love that you did all those things. It makes me feel ..."

He pulls me snugly against him again. "It makes you feel what?"

Loved.

The word echoes through my brain, but I know I can't say it. It's ridiculous to even think it, so saying it would be asinine. I'm not the kind of girl who thinks she loves a guy the first time they have sex. I didn't tell Freddy I loved him, and we dated for months.

Besides, I don't love Troy. I can't love Troy. I don't know him well enough to love him.

Don't be stupid, Dahlia.

"*Valued,*" I say, plucking a word out of the air. "It makes me feel valued."

"You should always feel valued."

I grin. "I really felt valued when you had your fist in my hair and was railing me from behind."

He chuckles. The sound makes my grin grow even bigger.

"What do you mean when you say this wasn't a hookup?" I ask, my stomach fluttering. "What does that look like?"

"It looks like if Theo calls you again to chitchat about Wednesday office snacks, he'll be eating his food through a fucking straw."

"Stop it," I say, laughing.

"I fucking mean it."

I lean up and scoot around so my back is on the other side of the tub and I'm facing Troy. He's not smiling, or laughing, or at all amused. And, my lord, *it's hot.*

"You can't do that," I say. "We work together. He's probably going to call me sometimes."

"And once he finds out you're mine, he better choose those calls carefully."

"*And once he finds out that you're mine ...*"

129

I shiver despite the warm water.

"What are we going to do about work?" I ask. "All joking aside. I haven't read the employee handbook about fraternization, but I'm assuming it's a no-no in our line of work."

He scoops up a handful of water and douses his face with it. I wonder if he's even considered it.

It's a huge potential problem, one I don't know how to manage. I know his loyalty lies with our boss, and I would never come between them. But I don't know where this leaves me. *Where does that leave ... this?*

Us?

The thought of having this time with Troy and returning to how we were is unbearable. Not when I've seen this side of him. Not when I've had him like this.

"I'm not putting you on the spot," I say. "I know this just happened, and we didn't plan it. I don't expect you to have all the answers because I sure as hell don't. But I think it would behoove us to figure it out as soon as possible."

He grins.

"What?" I ask.

"It *behooves us*. Who says that?"

I splash him. "Me, asshole."

He laughs, resting his arms along the sides of the tub. "I don't know what happens next. We'll figure it out. I'll talk to Ford. He may want to split us up or give me a more permanent position around the office."

"What if he splits us up, and Theo is my new guy?"

He smirks. "Theo will never be your guy. I can promise you that."

"You're awfully cocky, Mr. Castelli."

"Only when I know I'm right."

I move across the tub, planting my hands on the edge of the tub on either side of him, and kiss him. He wraps his arms around me, gripping my ass, and holds me in place.

Our mouths move effortlessly in sync.

I settle back between his legs again, my back to his front.

"So I can consider myself your girlfriend now? Is that what you're saying?" I ask cheekily.

"You can consider yourself whatever you want as long as it means no one else gets to have you."

"What if you decide a few days from now you aren't into this?"

"Doll, I've already been into you for two years. This just sealed the deal."

My cheeks ache from smiling. "So, boyfriend, tell me something about you."

"What do you want to know?"

I shrug. "Something I don't know. Something that will help me understand the enigma that is Troy Castelli."

"An enigma, huh?"

"I don't even know your middle name."

"Lucas. What's yours?"

"Penelope. It was my mom's name."

He kisses the top of my head. "It's beautiful, just like you."

I settle against him, relishing the contact.

We sit quietly for a long time, swaying in the water. A comfortable silence settles over the room.

I have so many questions for Troy Lucas Castelli. *Where does he see himself in five years? What did he love to do as a child? Does he want children?* But I don't want to push my luck—and I've been very lucky lately.

He bends his leg, exposing his knee through the water. I grab it to sit up when I notice a curious mark on his leg. I follow the raised scar with my fingertip.

"What's this from?" I ask. "Some kind of battle wound."

"You could say that."

"Is there a story behind it? Usually, guys have a legendary tale about these things. Like they found a lion or killed a shark."

"That's pretty accurate."

I laugh. "I figured."

"Only the monster was named my dad."

I freeze, replaying that again. *"Only the monster was named my dad."*

My throat tightens while my brain kicks into high gear. *What does that mean?*

"Well, I guess I know about your family, so you should know about mine," he says, the words flat and hollow.

He laces our fingers together and sighs.

"You don't have to tell me anything you don't want to," I say, squeezing his hand.

He sighs again, longer this time, and rests his head against the wall.

"The day my parents brought Travis home from the hospital ... I was so excited," he says. "I was five. I just got home from kindergarten. I'd walked the half mile in the pouring rain. Well, I ran the last half of it because Mom and the baby were supposed to be there, and I couldn't wait to see them. I had this idea in my head that when they got home, everything would be better."

I bring his arms around me and pin them to my chest. "You walked half of a mile by yourself as a five-year-old?"

"Crazy, huh?"

"I ... don't know what to say."

"Don't say anything yet because things did not get better," he says with a sad laugh. "As a matter of fact, they got worse. They fought constantly. These screaming arguments that resulted in something being thrown. I was always happy when it was a lamp or picture instead of Dad's fists."

Oh my God.

"Of course, the screaming would wake the baby, and then he'd start crying. And the crying would set my father off about how he didn't want fucking kids, and he'd flip furniture or throw a beer bottle across the room. I learned pretty quickly how to make a bottle and change diapers because I was scared to death that Dad was going to hurt Trav. And Trav didn't deserve it." He pauses, taking a deep breath. "Just like I didn't deserve it."

Tears pool in my eyes as I imagine what that must've been like. How scared he must have been. The thought of a baby Troy ... *I can't.*

Emotions clog my throat as I wait for him to continue. I can't ask questions because, if I do, I'll cry. And I'm pretty sure if I cry, he'll shut down. Instead, I squeeze his arms as tightly as possible to let him know I'm here.

I don't know what else to do.

"I took a lot of fucking beatings for that boy," he says, chuckling angrily. "It got worse as we got older. Dad would come home high as fuck or drunk or both and just hit the first thing he saw, which was usually me. Because if it was me, it wasn't my mom or my little brother."

"*Troy* ..." Tears stream down my face as my heart breaks. "I'm so sorry that happened to you."

"He tore Mom down until she was a shell of a human being. She just stayed in her room most of my childhood. We had a neighbor, Mrs. Autumn, who would leave sandwiches on her porch for Travis and me. She'd visit her sister for a couple of weeks every summer. Those were some hungry fucking weeks, let me tell you."

My body shakes as I hiccup back sobs.

"To this day, Travis gulps his food down." He laughs softly. "It's incredibly disgusting. Once, our house got stormed by ... hell, I don't know who it was. But Dad owed them money. That was the first time I had a gun held to my head. I was fourteen."

I don't know what to say. Nothing I can say will make it better. And the feeling of helplessness is overwhelming.

"Then, one day, it was late summer, and school was about to start. I had just turned seventeen."

His words are too careful, too hollow. I brace myself for whatever's about to come.

"Travis and I had been fishing with some friends. We pulled into the driveway and could hear them fighting. We go on in because there's no telling when it would end. You couldn't base your life around their fights. And it was ... *bad*."

He tightens his arms around me.

"Mom was bleeding from her nose. She had a cut down the side of her face. Dad had a broken beer bottle in his hand like he was going to slice her with it." His breathing grows rapidly. "I told Travis to go ... to get outside and stay there. There was a look in Dad's eye that just ... it was like he was gone. They were vacant. There was no sense of humanity or connection. It was the coldest thing I've ever seen."

He swallows hard.

"I was scared that day. Mom looked at me with just ... *terror* on her face. It was like she regretted every decision she'd ever made at that moment. And she told me to get out. To go with Trav."

"Did you?" I whisper, my tears dripping into the water.

"I think I knew what was going to happen," he says. "I don't know if it had been building up to that or if it was just the look on his face. But I knew he was going to kill her."

"*Troy.*"

"I jumped in front of her. He swung the bottle over me somehow, and it sliced her. Blood went everywhere," he says, his voice void of emotion. "I wrestled Dad to the ground. But he was over two hundred pounds, and I probably weighed a buck fifty. There wasn't a lot I could do."

I cover my mouth to keep the gasp on my tongue from escaping. He doesn't need my dramatics right now. He needs me to be strong for him.

"Travis came in at some point and grabbed a dumbbell off the floor and smashed Dad with it." He pauses. "It probably saved my life."

"What happened?"

"Travis needed therapy. I got a scar and probably need therapy, too. Dad went to prison, where he sits, rotting away in a cell." His voice cracks. "And my mother died in a pool of blood in my lap that day. And there wasn't a damn thing I could do about it."

"*Oh my God.*"

I break free of his grip and turn to face him. Tears stream down his face. I wipe them away with my thumbs.

My heart shatters into a million pieces at the sight of this strong, beautiful, amazing man crying because of something so incredibly unfair.

"I'm so sorry," I say, through my own tears. I wrap my arms around his neck and pull him into me. "I am so sorry."

He presses a kiss below my ear and holds me tight.

We sit that way until the water grows cold—until my teeth chatter from the chill.

"There you go," he says, pulling away. He tries to laugh to make light of the situation, but nothing is light about it. "Now you know a lot about me you didn't know before."

"I know that was hard for you. It means a lot that you shared that with me."

"Even though I made you cry?"

I smile at him, touching the side of his face. "What do you say we get out of this water and back into bed? I saw you got a frozen pizza in your grocery order. Let's put that in the oven and watch a movie."

He kisses me softly. "Thank you."

"Anytime."

We climb out of the water, and he wraps me in a fluffy towel. He holds my gaze as he fashions one around his waist.

No words are exchanged, but none are required.

Troy just trusted me. That says it all.

Chapter Sixteen

Troy

"Is this not the cutest place you've ever seen in your life?" Dahlia asks, climbing out of the car.

"I'm wowed."

She gives me a look, warning me to play along.

"Look," I say, shutting her car door for her, "I'd rather be at the house balls deep inside you. I'm sorry if this little village thing isn't as impressive as your pussy. Sue me."

She places her arms over my shoulders, her fingers dangling behind me. She lifts her chin and gazes wickedly into my eyes.

"If you play nice and pretend to be wowed," she says, biting her lip. "I'll wow you when we get back."

I push my cock against her. "I'm ready."

"How do you get hard that fast?" She laughs.

"Says the woman who gets wet at the drop of a hat."

I reach between her legs, but she swats my hand away, laughing harder. "Stop it."

"Why?" I pull her to me, nuzzling the crook of her neck. "Are you wet for me?"

She groans as I press kisses behind her ear. "You don't play fair."

"Is that a yes then?"

"Yes," she says, shoving me away. Her smile stretches across her pretty face. "I'm wet for you. I'm breathing, aren't I?"

"God, you turn me on."

She takes my hand, and I reluctantly follow.

I'll never admit it to her, but the town is cute. It looks like something from a movie set. Granted, it would be a Christmas movie with a yuppie with a bad haircut and a baker who wants to save the town's Christmas tree farm—but a movie all the same.

Every building is crafted to the smallest detail. The roads are meticulous, the shops are charming, and the fastidiously maintained landscape almost doesn't look real.

"Thank you for bringing me here, even though I know it's killing you," she says, leading me onto a sidewalk.

"If someone tries to kill you, maybe they'll shoot me first and put me out of my misery."

She gasps. "Not funny."

"It's funny when you joke about it."

"Because I'm the intended victim."

"Not in my scenario."

"Shut up," she says, pausing in front of an old-fashioned ice cream shop. "Is that not adorable?"

"It looks like a dollhouse."

"The dollhouse of my dreams." She looks at me. "They boast forty-eight handcrafted flavors. How do you come up with forty-eight flavors that aren't redundant?"

"Easy. Work through the vanilla variations, then the chocolate ones. Toss a pistachio in there, a buttered pecan. That's a personal favorite," I say as we move along down the sidewalk. "You can't forget the coffee flavor, and a classic bubble gum. There's mint and cheesecake. What about red velvet cake?"

She looks at me like I've lost my mind.

"What? You asked," I say.

"Sometimes, I can't get a word out of you. Other times, you surprise me with the strangest rambles."

"I like ice cream, okay?"

"Noted. Hey, there's a bookstore. Should we drop in and take a look?"

"I'll never say no to a good bookstore."

We cross the mostly vacant street thanks to the weather. The sky is dreary, threatening to drop bucket loads of water on our heads at any moment. It's the only reason I gave in to her request to visit the shopping center. I didn't think anyone else would be dumb enough to be out.

"Hang on," I say, digging my phone out of my pocket. I look at the screen. "It's Ford."

"Take it. I'll wait."

I kiss her forehead and answer the call. "Castelli."

"Hey," he says, his words clipped. "I have news."

My stomach tightens. I try to remain passive and not put Dahlia on edge.

"Shoot," I say.

"Dahlia's ex-boyfriend Freddy was arrested last night."

"Really? Why?"

"What's going on?" Dahlia asks, stepping to me. "I can see it on your face."

Dammit.

"Can she hear me?" Ford asks. "Can you put her on speakerphone?"

I look around and spot an empty grass lot next to the bookstore. "Hang on a second."

Dahlia follows me across the street, away from the sidewalk. Not a soul is around, so I press the speaker button.

"Okay," I say. "She can hear you."

"Hi, Ford," Dahlia says.

"Hey. So Freddy was arrested last night."

Her eyes widen. "Why?"

Ford blows out a breath. "He beat up your neighbor Burt."

"*What?*"

"Shhh ..." I say, making sure no one overheard her.

"*Oh my God.* He beat up Burt?" She takes my phone from me and holds it to her mouth. "Is he okay? What the hell happened?"

She looks at me helplessly. I pull her into my side. It's all I can do.

"Apparently, Freddy was at your house milling around," Ford tells her. "And Burt came out on his porch and confronted him."

"Oh no," she says, her shoulders falling.

"Burt had already called 911 before he went outside, so the police were already on their way. In retrospect, that might have saved his life."

Dahlia's hand goes over her mouth. "I can't ... Is Burt okay?"

"He'll live. Lacerations to the face and hands. A broken rib. Two black eyes. The police picked Freddy up a street over and charged him with resisting arrest, assault, and possession of drugs. Other charges are pending."

"Is Freddy in jail?" I ask.

"He bonded out this morning."

Dahlia's eyes squeeze closed, and I think she whispers a prayer. I take the phone from her. She gives it up without a fight.

"This is my fault," she says.

"*This is not your fault.*" I lift her chin so she has to look at me. "I mean it. Not your fault."

Her eyes are cloudy with tears, and I hate it. Even more, I hate the motherfucker who's doing this to her—and who hurt a poor old man.

"So Freddy is losing his shit," I say. "Are we thinking he's responsible for all of this?"

Ford takes a breath. "Actually, no. I have a bit more news on that front."

Dark clouds roll across the sky as thunder rolls in the distance.

"We've been able to trace the IP address from the email you

received with the pictures," Ford says. "We thought there would be a VPN on it to block the sender's location, but there wasn't."

Dahlia looks at me warily. "Who sent it?"

"It came from your father's house."

Fucking hell. I run a hand over the top of my head in frustration.

"What?" she asks, struggling to accept this information. "Are you sure?"

"We're sure. Can you tell us who frequents his house? Who would be there using their internet connection?"

She shakes her head as if trying to rattle herself awake. "Um, I don't know, really. I've only been there a few times. My father, obviously. Alexis. They have staff, but I don't know who they are or how many."

I grab her hand and hold it tightly.

"We did a little digging, and Alexis was in New Orleans the day you received the email. Unless she scheduled it previously, she wasn't home to hit send."

Dahlia takes my phone again, pacing a small circle.

I wish we were at the house so we could sit. I never should've brought her here.

"So what are you thinking?" I ask Ford.

"Is Alexis into photography?" he asks. "Does she have a lot of time on her hands to follow you around?"

"I have no idea if she's into photography or not," Dahlia says. "I assume she has more time than usual, considering my father is in his office or court these days. But I don't really know."

Ford clears his throat. "What about your father?"

She stops in her tracks. "He has no time to do it. And why? Why would he threaten to kill me? He's the one who initiated our relationship. If he didn't want me around, he could've stayed in the shadows forever."

"Maybe he thinks that shit is going to hit the fan with his trial, and he wanted you scared enough that you'd leave," Ford suggests.

"Couldn't he have just asked?" Dahlia laughs in disbelief. "It would've been a lot easier than to go through all this trouble, don't you think?"

Anger flashes in her eyes. It's the look of a woman who's not being heard.

If her gut tells her it's not her dad ... I'll run with that.

I'll make sure she's heard.

"I think we might be getting fucked up," I say.

"About what?" Ford asks.

"We're tangling two things together that may not be associated."

"What do you mean?"

Dahlia stops moving and watches me.

"She got an email that threatened her, right?" I ask. "Fine. Someone sent that. We're focusing on her father only because of his reputation and because he's in a court battle right now with some pretty serious charges."

"Correct," Ford says.

I hold Dahlia's gaze. "Maybe we're wrong. Maybe the two aren't as connected as you think."

A slow smile slips across her face.

"Occam's razor," Ford says. "The simplest solution is the common denominator. Joseph Dallo."

"There are exceptions to every rule." I grin back at her. "Look, you know I respect you and will not tell you how to do your job. But I do ask, respectfully, that you look beyond Joseph Dallo. Dahlia knows him better than anyone and feels he's not involved. I think we should put stock in that."

"You know I respect the hell out of you, Troy. But I think, respectfully, that the man involved with the Magne has the highest probability of being guilty."

"That hasn't been proven."

Dahlia wraps her arms around my waist. I lean my cheek against her head.

I can't believe I'm going to bat for a man I don't know—one I suspected yesterday was the perpetrator. *Have I completely lost it?*

"Thank you," Dahlia mouths to me.

Or did I just jump without a parachute?

I look at the sky, shaking my head. *Fuck you, Lincoln.*

"All right," Ford says. "Let me find out who else has access to Dallo's Wi-Fi and might want Dahlia dead."

"*Ouch.*" She makes a face. "That was harsh."

"Thanks, Ford." I wink at my girl. "I owe you one."

He laughs. "Troy, I owe you so many that we'll never get even."

"Let me know if you have any updates," I say.

"You got it. Talk to you soon."

"Thanks, Ford," Dahlia says.

"Stay safe. We'll see you back here before you know it."

"Later." I end the call.

Dahlia heaves a breath as I slide my phone back into my pocket. "I feel so bad about Burt."

"Yeah, I know. We'll make it up to him when we return to town."

"*We?*"

"Hey, he just fought on behalf of my lady. I'm indebted to him."

She grins. "I'm your lady, huh?"

"Is that okay?"

"I'll be whatever you want me to be as long as it means you're mine."

I pull her to me and kiss the tip of her nose. Surely, she knows I'm hers, even if she doesn't want me.

Nothing has ever made sense before. I've never met another person that I felt like truly gave a single shit about me. No one wanted to listen to anything I had to say. Most people never really see you, and if they do, it's to see what you have of value they can take away.

Not Dahlia.

She asks for nothing but honesty. She goes out of her way to make me smile. I've given her a hard time for two years, and the woman still shows up for me.

She gets angry when she thinks I'm being treated unfairly.

She trusts me to keep her safe.

She gives me space to tell her my secrets and holds me when I fucking cry without judgment.

Dahlia gives me her body, her heart—her laughter and her smiles.

I don't have as much to give her, and what I do is broken and rusty. But it's hers if she wants it.

And I hope to hell she does.

Because for the first time in my thirty-seven years on this planet, my future means more than my past.

I didn't think that was possible.

But I also didn't think it was possible to fall in love, and I've done that.

Chapter Seventeen

Dahlia

I wipe the counters and toss the sponge in the sink.

Dinner was simple yet delicious. We stopped at the village's small grocery store before returning earlier this afternoon. Troy grilled burgers while I threw some fries into the air fryer. We had a glass of wine and sat outside on the patio, talking and laughing.

It was anything but exciting. It was a run-of-the-mill, everyday experience—and it was so perfect that I'm not sure any day will ever top it. Just as I imagined, the more time we spend together, the more he's showing his true character. Even though he'll probably never use an emoji in a text message, and I'll always want to throttle him at least once a day, he's so worth it. I've seen more hints of his dry humor, thoughtfulness, and the sweet side of his personality that he keeps hidden.

I like the man. I like him a whole lot.

The weather was beautiful after the storms. Troy was the most carefree that I've ever seen him. And, despite my concern for Burt and curiosity over the email's source, I was content.

I haven't been content in years.

Troy wanted to grab a shower after dinner, and I was happy to spend a bit of time alone. It gave me a few minutes to gather my thoughts and process Ford's news from earlier in the day. My heart warms when I remember Troy having my back and encouraging our boss to look beyond my dad.

He didn't have to do that. And it means so much that he did.

I refill our wineglasses, then stop in our bedroom and quickly rinse off. Then I set off to look for my man. I find him on the balcony, lost in thought.

"Hey," I say as the breeze ruffles the edge of my pink silk robe. "What are you doing out here all by yourself?"

"Thinking that the only thing better than being out here alone is if I was out here with you."

I smile, setting our glasses on the small table between the two chairs.

The ocean laps against the beach on the other side of the gate below. The moon hangs high in the sky, the light twinkling off the water. A million stars dot the night and glitter overhead.

"You, Mr. Castelli, are gorgeous," I say, feathering his short hair with my fingers. He smiles, his perfect white teeth set off by his tanned skin. "I like many things about you, but right now, it's all superficial."

He chuckles, taking my hand and tugging me toward him.

A light switches on at the neighbor's house. Their balcony door opens, and a man's voice, while muffled, is audible. There's too much foliage to get a clear shot of the house, but shadows make me think someone else is watching the ocean, too.

I tug the piece of silk that closes my robe. The robe falls open, exposing my naked body beneath.

The air is warm and humid, and a sheen of moisture shines on my skin.

Troy grips the backs of my thighs and pulls me to him, sucking a nipple into his mouth. I reach around and rub the back of his neck.

"That feels so good," I say as he palms my other breast.

He flicks my nipple with his tongue, sending spikes of pleasure pulsing through my body.

"I think if you did that long enough, I might come," I say, absorbing every lick and nibble. "One day, we're going to try that."

He pulls away and grins. "Name the place and time."

"Not now." I take a step back and grab my drink. "I have something else I want to do."

His curiosity is piqued. "Do tell."

I down half my wine and motion for him to stand.

He follows my lead, downing half his wine, and then getting to his feet.

I slide my fingers beneath the band of his boxers and shove them over his hips.

"Oh," he says, kicking them off. "I think I like where this is headed."

"You will. I promise."

He chuckles. "I'm standing here naked while another man sits on his balcony, probably clothed, about thirty feet away."

"I hope he likes what he sees," I say, confident the man can't see us. Given the past few days, this should terrify me. But here, with Troy, I know I'm safe. He would absolutely not allow this if there was any danger. Any chance of being seen. It's partly why I find him so hot.

Troy's brows pull together as I drop to my knees. Once I'm looking up at him through my lashes, his eyes darken. I take the elastic off my wrist and pull my hair out of my face.

His cock is hard, already ready for me.

"Will you come in my mouth?" I ask. "I want to taste you."

"My God, Doll. Are you fucking kidding me?"

I giggle and wrap my hand around the base. Holding his gaze, I squeeze my way to the top. A bead of pre-cum dots the head, and I swipe it away with my thumb.

His eyes widen as he watches. His jaw is slack with anticipation.

I wipe my thumb slowly across my bottom lip, leaving a trail of his taste behind. Troy inhales deeply, not missing a beat.

"Remember how I once told you I was getting you right where I wanted you?" I ask.

He nods.

"This is where I wanted you." I lick the saltiness off my lip and then rise on my knees. "I want to do a good job for you. You have to tell me what you like."

"I'm not sure there's a damn thing you could do to me that I wouldn't like."

Granules of sand dust the floor, and they dig into my knees, but nothing will deny me this pleasure. I drag the backs of my fingers lightly up Troy's length, listening to him hiss in response.

"You're going to be the end of me," he says.

I gaze up at him, flicking the tip of his cock with my tongue. The hunger in his eyes makes me wet. My thighs are coated with my juices—that's how turned on I am, and I've barely started.

"I'm so wet right now," I say, laughing before placing kisses all over him. Some are quick pecks, and others are wet, sloppy ones. I mix it up to keep him guessing.

"You're always wet."

"Have you seen you?"

He chuckles, the sound cut short by a hiss as I lick my way from his balls to the tip of his cock in one slow, continuous motion. He cups my tits and squeezes them. His cock swells in response.

"Is someone over there?" a voice calls from the distance.

Troy looks over his shoulder as I take him down my throat. He grips the railing to keep himself steady, huffing a breath as he shudders.

"Hello?" the voice calls again. "Is that you, Landry?"

"Hey," Troy calls, the words tight as I suck my way up, flicking the head, and then slowly take him deep again. "No, this isn't Lincoln." He lowers his voice. "*Damn you.*"

147

I giggle, grabbing his balls with one hand and pumping his shaft with the other.

"I'm sorry," the man says. "Who are you?"

"I'm a part of Lincoln's security. We're doing some maintenance *over here.*"

The sentence ends an octave too high as I suck the head like a lollipop.

"Yeah, yeah," the neighbor says. "I know Grey. We shoot the shit sometimes."

"Yeah," Troy replies, sucking in a breath. "Yeah, that sounds like Grey."

He grips both sides of my head and holds me in place.

My spit slides down his cock, dripping over my hand and onto my chest. I look up at him, running my tongue over the head, and wait for him to tell me what to do.

"Do you want your little mouth fucked?" he asks, his eyes twinkling with mischief. "Is that what you want?"

I nod slowly, grinning.

Troy winds his fingers through my hair so tightly that I gasp. He thrusts his cock past my lips and then slides back out.

"*Good,*" he says softly. "That's what I like."

He pushes into my mouth again, holding my head in place.

A breeze whips across the balcony, knocking my robe off my shoulder. I suck my spit as best as I can, but most of it runs down onto my hands as I tug gently on his balls.

He moans as he pumps into my mouth. This time, it goes a little farther, hitting the back of my throat. I gag.

"Come on," he says, easing but not stopping. "You can take it. I know you can."

Oh shit.

I slurp around him, my breaths coming out in short bursts. His gaze is hot as he watches me take him in. It's the height of arousal, the one thing that makes me needier than anything else—knowing I'm the object of his pleasure.

He presses harder, deeper into my mouth.

"I'm going to come," he says.

I tug on his balls again, making him groan.

"If you don't want this in your mouth, tell me now."

Instead of telling him I don't want it, I position myself to take even more.

He groans, his cock swelling between my lips as his body begins to shake.

I moan around him, digging my nails into his ass.

"Be ready to swallow, Doll." He sucks in a breath. "*Motherfucker.*"

His body tenses and trembles as he shoots his cum down the back of my throat. My eyes burn as I accept it all, unable to pull away.

Not that I want to. This is the best seat in the house.

Troy's chin is aimed toward the sky, his Adam's apple bobbing as he strains from the force of his orgasm. It is, without a doubt, the absolute sexiest thing I've ever seen.

After a final full-body shiver, he slides out of my mouth.

"*Damn,*" he says, releasing my hair. He chuckles. "I just came so hard I can't see straight."

I laugh, wiping my mouth with the back of my hand.

He helps me to my feet.

"Are you still there?" the neighbor shouts.

"I gotta go take care of something," Troy yells. "It was nice talking with you."

"Yeah, you, too. Enjoy your stay."

Troy grins at me. "I have enjoyed my stay. And now you're about to enjoy yours." He scoops me up and hustles me inside.

My stomach clenches as I wonder what he's going to do. I know what I want him to do.

I pant as he carries me into the room closest to the patio—an office. He flips on a light, surveys the scene, and swipes everything to one side with his forearm.

Holy shit.

"Here you go," he says, setting me on the desk.

I laugh. "Do you even know whose desk this is?"

"Nope. Don't care." He smirks. "But you're about to come all over it."

Oh fuck.

My core tenses as a shot of adrenaline spikes in my veins. Troy lays me back, then drags my ass to the edge of the desk.

The desktop is cool against my skin. I shiver as I look between my knees. *How does he seem even more attractive to me right now?*

"Tell me what you like," he says, his eyes blazing. "I need you to feel as good as you just made me feel."

He spreads my knees to the sides, then extends one leg. His eyes on mine, he plants kisses down the inside of my leg. The closer he gets to my pussy, the slower the kisses become.

"I'm literally so worked up right now that if you touch my clit, I'll probably die," I say.

He chuckles against my thigh. "Better not do that yet, then."

"No, you should. Like now."

I reach to touch myself, but he captures my wrist.

"Don't." He blows across my pussy, making me writhe on the desk. "You don't come until I say you do."

"How is that fair?'

"It's not. But that's the game we're playing."

I laugh through my frustration. "Wait until the next time I'm in control of the game and see what happens."

He licks up my other thigh, making me moan.

"Doll, you're never in control, but it's cute that you think you are."

"Keep talking shit, and you won't touch my pussy."

He laughs. "One of us is shit-talking right now. The one dripping all over Lincoln Landry's desk."

"I—*oh fuck.*"

Troy's tongue touches the bottom of my slit, making me quiver. He drags the tip of his tongue through my wetness and over my clit.

I sag against the desk. *Dammit.*

"You're literally making me crazy," I say, pouting. "I didn't torture you. I let you—*yes!*"

I sigh in relief as he repeats the process with a little more pressure.

"Please," I beg. *"Please, please, please.* Don't stop this time."

I'm desperate for a release. I need to unwind this ball that's bound so tightly it hurts.

He licks my pussy but goes nowhere near my clit. The swollen bud aches, craving his attention. But the asshole ignores it like he doesn't know what he's doing.

I know that's a fucking lie.

He dips his tongue inside me, adding a finger at the last minute. I groan in desperation.

"Why do you hate me?" I ask, fake crying.

"I don't hate you. Do you think I'd bury my face inside someone I hated?"

I run my hands over his head. "I'm not sure. It might be possible."

He laughs, going back to torturing me.

Troy's not in a hurry. None of my protests speed him up. In fact, the more I beg, the slower I think he goes.

He licks and sucks, strumming his fingers inside me like he's playing an instrument. Each touch, each swipe of his tongue, sends shots of unsatiated need barreling through me.

"I can't," I say, my eyes squeezing shut. "I just need to—*ah!*"

My lungs release air in a steady moan as he licks circles around my clit. Each flick of his tongue over the sensitive spot sends a shock straight into my core.

"Is that better?" he asks, grinning against my flesh. "You're complaining a hell of a lot less."

"You're an asshole."

"Keep it up, and I'll fuck that, too."

I don't tell him that I'm so wound up that I might just let him if he asks.

I shift against the desk, my ass sticking to the wood. The sound of my skin peeling away from the desktop slices through the room.

"Please let me come," I say, whimpering.

I'm shaking uncontrollably. My legs tremble. I'm so close. *Almost there.*

"You're beautiful," he says, sucking my bud into his mouth.

I moan, unable to control the volume. My voice fills the room, rising over the sound of Troy licking my pussy.

He increases the speed of his assault. I'm panting for dear life, barely able to keep my eyes open. I grab his head and pull it into my body, spreading my knees as wide as they'll go.

Two fingers slide inside me, twisting as he pulls them out.

"*Troy* ..."

His name is a shaky, three-syllable word as I teeter on the edge.

"Look at me," he says. When I don't, he stops all movement. "*Look at me.*"

I breathe, opening my eyes, and they immediately find his.

He smirks, dropping his face to my pussy again, and plunges his fingers deep inside me.

I gasp as he presses his tongue against my clit.

I shriek when he doesn't stop.

I tremble on his tongue as he gives me what I've asked for—and makes me come in his mouth.

"Oh my God!" I yell, unable to stop myself from shaking. "Fuck you!"

My hips lift, and my thighs try to press together, but he refuses to move. The orgasm is too powerful. The strength of the climax is too much.

The room fades away, and I'm unsure if I'm floating or still on the desk. I'm not even sure where he's touching me anymore. It feels like he's everywhere.

"I can't ... Troy! *I can't.*"

"*Yes, you can,*" he says, milking my orgasm for me. "Stop fighting me."

The intensity begins to wane, and my vision slowly returns. The room isn't a blur anymore. I go limp.

Troy stands, his face glistening with my cum. He smiles and shakes his head.

"What?" I ask, too tired to even sit up.

"That was the most typical Dahlia thing I've ever witnessed."

I hum, too exhausted to care what he's talking about.

"You beg me to eat your pussy, then you fight me when it gets good." He scoops me up in his arms. "That's such a *you* thing to do."

"A *me* thing to do right now is to take a nap."

"Let's clean up together, and then we'll lie down."

I run my finger along his jaw, my heart filled with adoration for him. "Sounds like a plan."

He gives me his new shy smile and carries me away.

Chapter Eighteen

Troy

Sleep has never been a friend of mine.

I can't remember a time in my life when rest came easy. As a child, when the sun went down, things got sporty. Dad would come home and wake the whole house up with his yelling and breaking shit. If he was gone, the paper-thin walls would betray my mother's privacy, and Travis and I would hear her crying in her room. Ralph even knew. Once it got dark, he'd corral my brother and me into our shared closet of a bedroom and lay in front of the door.

And we waited.

It's been twenty years since I lived in that house—since I lived with, *since I had parents*—and I still fight anxiety every evening. Old habits die hard.

I exhale, blowing out some of the frustration riddling me tonight. I lie with Dahlia because she, too, seems to have a bad relationship with the dark. Something tells me this is a new thing with her, that it probably started once she realized her privacy had been violated. I don't ask. I can't track down the person who fucked with her and fuck with them back ... yet.

But I will.

I pick up my glass of tea that was hot an hour ago and carry it to the table. My computer's open, and a notepad and pen are beside it.

I'm particularly antsy tonight. Something's nagging at me, and I can't pinpoint it. I can't work through the fog to find the root of my disturbance.

"What the hell is bothering me?" I ask the empty room. "What am I missing?"

I consider that it's simply that I want to go home. I want to get it out of the way. When I think about returning to Savannah and all the things that could go wrong—assuming the stalker has been found and dismembered—it makes me nauseous ... and ready to fight. I'm already done. Dahlia stole my fucking heart when I didn't think I even had one. I've intentionally avoided this situation, this level of vulnerability, my entire life. Truth be told, it wasn't that hard.

Until her.

Fear coats my stomach, reminding me this could go wrong. I could fail her. *What if I'm unequipped to love her the way she wants to be loved?*

What if she realizes that I'm unlovable?

"Stop it," I say, admonishing myself. I sit at the table and awaken my computer. "I might be in Lincoln's house, but I don't have to be weak."

I skim over the spreadsheet I started earlier, listing everyone who could be behind Dahlia's threats. I'm missing something. I can feel it.

But what?

The list isn't too long, but it is complicated.

Joseph Dallo.

Someone from Alfred Dallo's (grandfather) past:

- Cartel connection

- Revenge
Someone at Joseph's house:
- Alexis Dallo
- Staff
Freddy Henke

I log in to the Landry Security system and pull up Dahlia's file. Clicking through the team's notes and logs, I don't find anything that stands out. I grit my teeth and open the pictures sent to her in the email.

"What can I learn from this?"

I zoom in on the image from her bathroom. *We know how this was taken. Theo found the camera.*

Thank fuck the bastard didn't send a naked picture of Dahlia. Because I'm sure he got some, given the angle.

I swipe to the shot of her at dinner with friends. Something about it bothers me. I lean forward, blowing it up, and then reduce it. The only thing I notice is how hot Dahlia looks in red lipstick.

"Why have I never seen her in red lipstick before?"

I move to the next image, but before it loads, I return to the previous picture.

"She's wearing red lipstick." I sit back in my chair. "You'd have to be reasonably close or have an expensive camera with a long-range lens to capture that."

All the photographs are in that vein. The grocery store. The park. At her friend's house.

"Someone wasn't too worried they'd be caught," I say. "If they were busted, they'd have had to have an excuse that would be believable."

They know her.

I flip back to the spreadsheet and put a strike-through next to the cartels. "That rules out the cartel connection. They just murder, anyway. They aren't going to go to all this trouble."

Then I strike the open category of revenge. It's too impersonal.

"What about Daddy Dearest?" I say, studying Joseph's name. "There are probably reasons I could pin it on you, but I ... *eh.*" I groan, shaking my head. "It doesn't make sense. Why wouldn't you have asked her to leave if you wanted her gone? And why would you have intentionally entered her life less than two years ago, just to threaten her life?"

I sigh, trying to be unbiased. *Maybe Ford knows something I don't.* That could be why he thinks he's a viable candidate for murder.

"Let's play devil's advocate," I say, working through it. "What would make a man flip that fast?"

I tap my fingertips on the table. *The only thing that could make me change my mind about anything is Dahlia.*

"Could be," I say. "If Alexis is unhappy, Joseph could want to back out of his relationship with his daughter. It's possible. Maybe telling her to run was supposed to be enough to make her flee?" I groan. "But she has contact with him. He calls her. It doesn't make sense."

I blow out a breath. "The email was sent from the Dallo house. So that brings us to Alexis and the staff. But she was gone the day the email was sent ... and why would the staff care?"

I strike the staff from the spreadsheet, along with Joseph and Alexis.

"And that leaves Freddy." I flip to the team's notes on the little bastard. "Finance graduate. Good family. Bit of a black sheep, but we all have one of those." I scroll through random shit that has the hall-marks of Theo written all over it. "Took a wrong turn about a year ago. He wanted Dahlia back. Ninety-three calls to her cell phone over the past seven days. Charges pending."

If he wanted her back, why would he threaten her? The odds don't favor her running to *him*. It doesn't make sense. Not really.

"But none of this makes fucking sense," I groan again, growing agitated. "What am I missing, dammit?"

I look back through the names and hover over Alexis Dallo.

"He says he fell in love with her at first sight. Her letter said he was the most handsome man she'd ever seen." Dahlia's words about her parents filter through my mind.

"When, exactly, did Joseph Dallo marry Alexis?" I ask, my finger-tips flying across the keyboard. Newspaper articles load in seconds. "Three years ago on July twenty-second."

My heart lodges in my throat as I search again. This time, it's for an obituary. "Penelope Lovelace died ..." I scroll down the page. *Fuck.* "Three years ago on March first."

I stare at the dates on the screen. "He waited until Penelope died before he married Alexis? That's either ironic or ... not."

Puzzle pieces snap together, but I don't have enough to see the entire picture. But I know from experience that when too many pieces go together too easily, it's because they belong there.

"This could mean that ole Joe was in love with Penelope and couldn't move on as long as she lived." I try to imagine being with another woman and knowing Dahlia walks the planet. "Definitely possible. Or it could mean ..."

I glance at the clock. It's late. Very late.

But fuck it. Ford knows how to silence a ringer if he doesn't want to be woken up.

It rings twice before he answers it. "Landry."

"Hey."

"What are you doing calling so late? Everything okay?"

"Can't sleep. The bed's too soft. You?"

"Can't sleep. No room. Ellie's currently lying across it diagonally."

I snort. "Can't you buy a bigger bed?"

"Man, she'll just jack that one, too. I love her, but she's like sleeping with an alligator who does the death spiral randomly through the night."

"Where do you sleep?" I ask.

"Couch."

"You don't have a guest room or something?"

Ford laughs. "I happily take the couch because that means she's in my bed. At the end of the day, that's all that matters."

I glance up the stairs and grin.

"Anyway, why are you calling me at four in the morning?" he asks.

"How hard have you looked into Alexis Dallo?"

"Her background report's squeaky clean. She's done community service out of the kindness of her heart. Has a degree in nursing but isn't using it right now. She was a pageant queen. I mean, she's basically the thirty-year-old version of an all-American girl."

I narrow my eyes, mulling this over again.

Thirty. She's only a few years older than Dahlia.

Would Alexis be jealous of her much older husband's love for a woman who's so close in age they could be sisters? Would it matter that Dahlia was his daughter?

I don't know. Some women, *insecure women*, can be petty over things like that. And Alexis isn't working, so she has time on her hands.

What if ... "I think you need to take a closer look."

"What's your working theory?"

I get to my feet and wander around the living room. The bookshelves lining the living room's far wall contain books, mementos, and pictures. Multiple framed images of Lincoln and his family fill nearly every empty space on the shelves. I can almost hear their laughter through the photographs, and I wonder what this house is like when they're all here.

Is something like that a possibility someday for a guy like me?

"Working theory," I say, refocusing. "Dallo married Alexis around four months after Dahlia's mom passed away."

"And?"

"I wonder if our blushing bride knew her sugar daddy already had a baby with someone else? Hadn't married anyone else until the love of his life passed away?"

"Okay ..."

"I can't ask Dahlia. She isn't going to know that, and I don't want to plant ideas in her head in case I'm wrong. If I'm completely off course, I won't ruin their relationship over a hunch."

"You know, it makes sense."

I nod. "Think about it. You're a beautiful thirty-year-old woman in the prime of your life. And you marry an old rich dude with no kids. I'm not saying she's a gold digger. But she didn't marry an old poor dude or an old rich dude with a great reputation."

"Then you marry him ..."

"And realize you're splitting the inheritance. You're riding that old cock for half."

Ford sighs. "You might be right."

"Wouldn't be the first time."

"You know, I've been considering scheduling a meeting with Dallo. He's busy, so he might not even want to see me. But let's bring him into the fold and see what shakes out. Let's see where his loyalties lie."

"I have one request."

"What might that be?"

I smile. "If he's behind this, you'll give me two minutes with him alone before you call the police."

"Go to bed. Get some sleep."

"Think of all the things I've done for your family. Remember Barrett's election and the fight at the farm? Or when Lincoln almost got rocked by Nate Hughes? Or when Graham tried to intimidate Walker Gibson *in a bar*?"

"Yeah, yeah, yeah."

"Two minutes, Landry, or we're done," I say, only half joking.

"Good night."

"Good night."

I end the call, shut my computer, and put my mug in the dishwasher. Then I go back to bed.

Dahlia sleeps peacefully, her sweet lips pressed together in a pout. I want to kiss them, but if I do, she'll wake up, and we'll fuck and ...

I climb in beside her and touch my lips to hers.

Her long lashes flutter awake, and a slow smile stretches across her pink cheeks when her eyes focus.

I'd do anything for this woman. I'd do anything to keep this smile on her face, this peace in her eyes. It's what I'm supposed to do. I don't know how I know that, but I do.

"What time is it?" she asks sleepily.

"About four."

"Why are you up? Everything okay?"

I pull her against me, tucking her head beneath my chin. "It is now."

"I was having a dream," she says.

"What was it about?"

"It's hard to explain."

I kiss the top of her head. "Was it a good one?"

She leans back, her eyes flickering in the dim moonlight. "It was a great one. Want me to show you?"

I roll her onto her back and hover over her. Her legs wrap around my waist, her arms dangling over my shoulders.

"How did you know?" she asks, giggling.

"It was a good guess."

I forget about my troubles and fears and what tomorrow might hold. Instead, I lose myself in Dahlia.

She might've been dreaming about this, but she *is* my dream.

I hope she understands that someday.

Chapter Nineteen

Dahlia

I climb the steps from the workout room, leaving Troy behind to run *another* five miles. I didn't even want to work out this morning, but I wasn't going to miss an opportunity to see him shirtless and sweating—even if that meant lifting weights because he says it's good for my bones. It won't be good for my bones if I drop one from fatigue and break my foot. But I didn't bring that up. I'll save that for a time when I need him moody.

Moody sex, I've learned, is the best.

I yawn, heading into the kitchen to make a cup of coffee. My dreams last night were actual nightmares—something I didn't tell Troy. For one, I'm starting to think he takes any discomfort or perceived unhappiness to heart as if it's his fault or responsibility.

That breaks my heart.

For two, I know the reason for the bad dreams is a nonissue. It's silly.

The man next door last night is not a threat. He had to have passed a background check to live here. They card every person coming onto the island and again to enter this neighborhood. He's lived here for who knows how long. It's not like he bought a house a day ago to stalk me. He even named-dropped Grey.

All that being said, I know that Troy would've been on top of things if he thought anything was even remotely amiss. He wouldn't get sidetracked by a blow job or a smooth-talking name-dropper, so I could largely *logic* away my anxiety. Still, I'm not sure my heartbeat ever slowed back to its baseline. Maybe it would *when this is all over*.

I pour myself a steaming cup of joe and add a little milk. But as soon as the acidity hits my stomach, I nearly vomit.

"You gotta love anxiety," I grumble, dumping the caffeine down the drain.

I sit at the table, feeling the warmth of the sunshine streaming through the windows, and think about Burt—the other part of my night of terrors. I kept seeing him bleeding, reaching his old, wrinkled hand to me, and begging me to help.

Tears fill my eyes. I ache for him. He didn't deserve Freddy's wrath ... and it's my fault. I brought Freddy into Burt's world. I literally hate myself for that.

My face heats as I consider calling him once again. The thought is a rock in my stomach, getting thrown around by the acid burning holes in my organs.

I know I shouldn't call him. I shouldn't turn my phone on. Ford downloaded the data from it and let me keep it just in case but was adamant I keep it off.

Besides, I know the drill. We deal with this every day.

My fingertips strum against the table.

Even if Freddy knew where I was, I'm nowhere near Savannah. And with charges against him, he can't even leave the state of Georgia.

The whole thing is overblown, anyway. He had a moment of empowerment and was going to scare me. But now that he's getting charged with resisting arrest, assault, and whatever else, I'm probably the least of his problems.

I bite my lip.

So one quick call to Burt wouldn't hurt, would it?

I press against my belly and feel it churn. It hurts. I probably have an ulcer already. And, most importantly, Burt is my *best neighbor.* He's probably lying in his hospital bed alone with no one visiting him and no one giving a crap.

Tears roll down my cheeks.

I move quickly before I can change my mind and hustle upstairs to my bag. I find my phone. With shaky hands, I hold the power button.

As soon as the lights come on, I know I've fucked up. But I'm already in it this far, so I might as well see it through.

Act now and repent later.

My battery indicator is red, so I ignore the missed calls and unread texts, find Burt's number, and hit *call.*

"Please pick up," I say, glancing at the doorway. "Come on."

"Hey, sweet pea."

I stifle a sob at the sound of his scratchy, raspy voice.

"*Burt.* Oh my gosh, it's good to hear your voice. I heard what happened. Are you okay?"

"Don't be sorry for me. I just got a broken rib or two." He stops to cough, wincing at the end. "I got a couple of good shots in on that little son of a bitch. And he got arrested, I heard."

"Are you in the hospital?"

"Yeah. Gonna keep me a couple of days. When you hit your seventies, they like to make you think you're on death's door. It's a little game they play. But, hell, there are three hots and a cot. I'll survive."

I laugh, wiping away my tears. He sounds good—weak and definitely groggy—but he still has his wit. That's a great sign.

"So where have you been?" he asks. "I've been worrying. You're never gone this long."

"I know, and I'm sorry. I'll be home soon, and I'm going to take care of you."

"The hell you are."

"I'm not scared of you," I say.

"Well, you should be. Just ask Freddy Fuckface."

I laugh. "Listen, I hate to get off here this fast, but I have to. I'll be unreachable for a couple more days. I'll be at your door as soon as I get home. Do you have my friend Morgan's number? Did she give it to you?"

"Yup. You know, I think she's hitting on me. She wants some of this grandpa juice."

I laugh again, relieved that he's still his ornery self, even if that last part was a bit nauseating. "You're probably right. But if you need anything at all, call her. She'll help you."

"Are there parameters on that? Like are you talking dinner or sponge baths?"

"Burt, behave." I pause. "And, Burt?"

"Yeah, sweet pea?"

"I'm so sorry." My voice cracks, heavy with sorrow and guilt. "I'm so sorry this happened to you. It's all my fault, and I—"

"Nah, I'm not listening to this bullshit. None of this was your fault. But I gotta go. Someone's standing over me with a needle."

"I'll see you very, very soon."

"Bye."

The call ends.

My heart pounds now that the deed is done, and all that's left is to face the music ... or Troy. And he's not exactly going to be a beautiful symphony over this.

It'll be more like a symphony of destruction.

I reach for the power button but hit the voice mailbox instead. The top message is from Joseph Dallo with a time stamp of this morning.

Curiosity gets the best of me, and I hit *play*. My hands are trembling, so I turn on the speakerphone.

"Hi, Dahlia, it's your dad. I've been trying to call you for a few days now. I hope you're okay. I just want to give you a heads-up that much is going to happen very soon. You might want to keep your head down for a while, just in case. I've spent my whole life trying to keep you safe, and I don't want to fail you now. This will be over soon. I promise."

I press the power button and turn to shove my phone back in my bag. But I only get partially turned when my gaze is met with a set of steely gray eyes.

My body runs hot. My cheeks flame. I try to control my breathing so I don't panic ... *because he's pissed.*

"What will be over soon?" he asks, his eyes blazing. "What the hell are you doing?"

"I can explain."

"You better do it quick."

I take a quick breath. "Troy, hear me out. I had to know how Burt was doing. It's all my fault, and I know it was stupid. But—"

"*You think?*"

He fills out the doorway with his towering body and powerful presence. I can't imagine being on his bad side and how terrifying that would be. But I'm not scared of him. Moreover, I know his reaction is because I'm on his good side.

"I can't help it," I say, holding my hands out in front of me. "He has no one, Troy. Not a soul on this planet to check on him, and I'm the reason he's hurt."

He snatches my phone out of my hand and slips it into his shorts pocket.

"Keep doing shit like this, and you'll be the reason *you're* hurt," he says, his jaw flexing. "You'll also be the reason I'm in fucking prison for murdering the person who hurts you." He groans, running a hand over his head. "How could you be so careless?"

I fight the tears that want to come. "This is hard for me, okay?"

"I understand that. But you work for a security company. You know how phones are tracked. We say it all the time. Small mistakes make big problems. And this"—he removes my phone from his pocket and waves it in the air—"this is not a *small mistake.*"

"Be mad at me. I was careless. I know you're coming from a good place with this, and I screwed up," I say, fighting so hard not to break down in front of him. But the enormity of the past week just hit me like a ton of bricks, knocking me flat on my proverbial ass. "But I'm doing my best here not to panic, not to think, not to worry ... not to focus on the fact that someone wants to fucking kill me. And, in the meantime, my friend just got hurt, and I'm his only friend, and ... *I'm having a hard time today, okay?*"

Tears spill down my cheeks as I step away from him.

He bristles, his breathing turning ragged.

"When it was just me, it was fine," I say. "But it's hard to know that innocent people are paying the price for my life. For my choices. I'm the one who dated the asshole."

"I know all about how hard it is to live with things you probably caused."

I storm across the room, shoving my finger in his chest. He's a blur through the tears that won't stop. "*You did not cause that.*"

He stiffens, reverting to the Troy I know at work—the one that puts up a shield when emotions are involved. The only sliver of the man I've known over the past few days is a softness buried in his eyes.

"Don't do this to me," I say, dropping my finger.

He ignores me, making sure my phone is off, and throws it on the bed. "Who was on the voicemail?"

I wipe my face with the backs of my hands. "My dad."

"What did he say?"

"I don't know. That this will be over soon, and that something's going to happen, and I need to keep my head down."

His anger at me slips. "What's that mean?"

"I don't know."

"What did he say? Say it again as close as you can remember it."

I sit on the bed, my shoulders sagging. *How did this day turn so quickly?*

Just an hour ago, we were in the gym laughing and lifting

weights. I was trying to barter blow jobs for fewer reps. He was promising orgasms for extra repetitions. And now, we're here.

Oh, how quickly things can change.

"*Dahlia.*"

I typically like to screw with him when he says my name like that —demandingly. But I'm not in the mood for one. And I have a feeling this isn't going to end in moody sex.

"Okay," I say, gathering myself. "He said he hopes I'm okay and that something will be happening very soon, and I should keep my head down for a while. Um ... something about he's spent his whole life trying to keep me safe, and he doesn't want to *fail you* now. And it'll all be over soon."

Troy stands tall, his eyes dark. "I need to make some calls. Please don't put out an SOS or anything while I'm gone."

"*Troy ...*"

For the first time, he doesn't look back.

Chapter Twenty

D ahlia

Rain pelts the roof, and bolts of lightning crack through the sky almost continuously. A chilly breeze blows through the room, causing the floor-to-ceiling curtains to dance. It's the perfect day to curl up with a book and nap the day away. I've tried. After Troy disappeared from the bedroom and didn't come back, I fled to the third story and tucked myself away in the screened-in room.

A soft blanket covers my legs, and a book lays on my lap. I found it on a shelf in the living room. It looks good, a sports romance of all things, but I can't get into it. My real-life hero is somewhere in this house and isn't talking to me.

I don't blame him.

Calling Burt was reckless. I understand my emotional response and give myself grace for it, but I can't excuse putting us both in danger—no matter what.

If something were to happen to Troy because of me ...

I take a deep breath to steady myself and to offset the panic rising quickly inside me. I can't go there. I can't think about something happening to him.

Not when we're just getting started.

My instinct is to find him and apologize and to try to make things right. I know I was wrong. But I don't know him well enough like this —not yet—to know if he needs time to calm down, or if he needs me to go to him.

The unknowing hurts. A lot. Because all I want to do is be his partner, but that requires knowing the other person intimately. And, obviously, I don't.

I close my eyes, resting my head against the back of the sofa and wish this mess was over.

But somehow, I got to keep him.

"Hey."

My head snaps up, and my heart springs to life. The sight of him leaning against the doorjamb, hands in his pockets—his eyes sad and weary—shatters my heart.

"Hey," I say carefully, setting the book on the end table. "I was going to find you, but I thought maybe you needed some time to cool off."

"I yelled at you."

It's a simple sentence that's anything but that. It's a confession of his worst fears, an admission of wrongdoing—it's a forlorn acknowledgment that he's accepted defeat. All I can think about is the comparison he must be making between himself and his father … because he was upset.

Oh, Troy.

"You didn't yell at me," I say softly. "We were having a heated, *serious* conversation. It's okay."

"I don't want to yell at you. I don't want it to be like that."

I gulp back a wave of emotions and pull my blanket back. "Come here. Please."

He trudges across the room and sits beside me, so I crawl into his lap. His shoulders slump as he wraps his arms around me and holds me tightly, burying his face in my hair.

"Do you know how I know it'll never be like that?" I ask.

"How?"

"Because it kills you to think you hurt me. Even though you didn't. And I know your heart, Troy Lucas Castelli, and you wouldn't hurt me. You'd die first."

He sighs, planting kisses on the top of my head. "I'm sorry, Doll."

"For what? For being upset that I did something stupid? No. *I'm sorry.* I let my fear and emotions get the best of me, which was irresponsible."

"All I could think about when I saw you on your phone was someone on their way to hurt you. And I just ... dammit, Dahlia. I can't even think about it."

"And I can't think about anything happening to you, and to know I was so selfish today just ..."

My lips tremble as I struggle against the tears.

He blows out a long, tired breath.

"I just want to protect you and make you happy," he says. "And I worry I can't do that. I worry I can't keep you safe, and you'll see that I'm a fraud."

"What?" I pull away from him so I can see his face. "I'm the safest when I'm with you. I'm the happiest when we're together. Don't you understand that? These past few days have been stressful, sure, but I've smiled more, laughed more ... and felt taken care of in a way I never have before. *And that's because of you.*"

His eyes fill with relief, and he settles back against the couch. "Are relationships always this stressful?" He chuckles. "I've never thought much about it. I've never been interested in it. But now I realize that it hurts me more when you're upset than it does when I'm upset. And, when you think about it like that, why do people do this?"

"What are you saying? That you don't want to do this?"

He laughs, pulling me into him again. "*Right.*"

We sit quietly for a long time, listening to the storm rage outside. I want to ask him if we have to leave now that I've screwed up—but I don't. Because the thought of leaving our little cocoon is depressing.

Troy must be thinking the same thing because he sighs.

"I told Ford what happened today," he says. "I'm waiting to hear what he wants to do."

"What do you think he'll do?" I sit up and pull the blanket over me again. "You know what? I say we go back."

"No."

"Landry Security is wasting so many resources on this. You're wasting so much time."

"Not what I would call it."

I roll my eyes. "This is why I didn't want to tell you guys to start with. I knew you'd overreact."

"You haven't seen overreacting yet."

"*Please.*"

He sits up, stretching his neck back and forth. I know this motion. I tease him about it in the office—that he's limbering up for a fight.

Only, here, it's just me. So ...

"Should I stretch?" I ask.

"What?"

"You're doing the neck thing."

He laughs, his chest shaking with the force. "I'm going to tell you something."

"Oh fuck."

"And you're going to listen and not panic and not start being bossy."

"I make absolutely no promises with those terms and conditions."

He shakes his head. "Ford's meeting with your father right now."

I spring off the couch. "What? Why's he doing that?"

My heart pounds. *Do they know something I don't? Was I wrong this whole time? What the heck have they been doing and not telling me—about my life?*

"I didn't want to tell you this because it's a theory." His voice is too calm like he's talking to a wounded badger. "But I had a thought last night when I was digging around while you slept, and Ford's checking it out today."

"With my dad?"

He nods carefully.

My hands fly to my hips. "What's the theory? And don't tell me you joined everyone else and think I'm being naive."

"No one thinks that."

"Yes, they do. And I even understand it a little bit. Joseph Dallo looks like a terrible person. I'd probably think I was naive, too. Except I know I'm not. And I know he's not behind this. Won't you guys just freaking believe me?"

He smirks. "Are you done?"

I lift my chin. "I don't know. Let me think about it."

"The theory is that it's Alexis."

My jaw drops to the floor. "Alexis?"

Troy nods.

I sit beside him and let my brain sort that out.

"Did she know about you when they got married?" he asks.

"Um, I don't know. I've never thought about it." I think back to the first few times I met them both. "Yeah, I don't know. We have a weird relationship, which I guess is to be expected. I can't really read whether she's just naturally a colder person or if she's just chilly to me. Why?"

"Well, your dad married Alexis just a couple of months after your mother died. And it hit me last night that maybe she didn't know about you, because you didn't know about them for another year and a half, right?"

I nod.

"She's thirty years old, Dahlia. She's dating a man in his sixties. Who had no kids until recently. And he is worth a lot of money if you believe even a fraction of the online guesstimates."

Wow. "Okay. You suspect she married my dad for his money,

thinking he was childless with a huge estate to go somewhere. So she marries him, plays the doting wife—"

"I'm not saying she's digging gold. She might really love your father. But people factor children into marriages every day, and there's not always that much coin on the line."

That's true.

"On another note," I say. "Can you imagine being as wealthy as my father and never being able to trust anyone? You'd second-guess literally everyone you come into contact with, wondering if they liked you or what you could do for them. That would be so crummy."

"Yeah. I don't have that problem. I know flat-out that you like me for my cock."

I snort. "Among other things."

"There are other things?"

"Yes. But your sparkling personality isn't one of them."

He grabs me, sets me on the couch, and then kneels between my legs. His elbows rest on my knees as he smirks up at me.

"I'm sorry," he says with complete genuineness. "I need to know this. I'm going to try to be the best man you've ever known."

I touch the side of his face. "You already are." I lower my mouth to his but pull back before he can deepen it. "And I need to know that you know that I don't expect you to be perfect. I'm obviously not."

We laugh together.

"And we're going to have arguments, Troy. And we're going to see things differently. And we're gonna fuck up. Probably you more than me."

I wink at him, making him laugh. The sound is music to my ears.

"We're going to have to trust each other," he says. "It's a big deal to me. More than most people, I think. I can't deal with people in my life who I can't trust."

"I understand. And I can't deal with people in my life who don't let me love them. It's a part of who I am."

A soft grin splits his cheeks.

"What?" I ask.

"Nothing."

"*No, what?*"

He shakes his head as if he's embarrassed. It's adorable, even if I don't understand it.

"So what do we do now?" I ask. "We're waiting for Ford to tell us if we can come home or need to stay on the run?"

"Yeah."

"What do you think he'll say?"

Troy shrugs. "I don't know. It depends on what happens in their meeting, I guess."

"What do you want to do?"

"Whatever keeps you safe. What do you want to do?"

I rest back on the couch and wonder what I'd choose if I could pick anything at all. *Would I go home? Would I stay here? Would I fly to a tropical location and drink cocktails out of pineapples?*

But as I imagine every scenario, they all have one thing in common. He's about six-three, with slate-gray eyes and a mouth that can perform magic. No matter where I see myself, I see him there, too.

"Do you know what I think?" I ask.

"No. What?"

"I think you're stuck with me, Mr. Castelli."

He smiles. "Do you know what I think?"

"No. What?"

"I wouldn't have it any other way."

My blood heats as I absorb the way he looks at me.

"I have an idea," I say.

"Tell me."

"How would you feel about ordering a pizza for dinner and just lying in bed for the rest of the day? We can watch a movie or, you know, you could find other ways to entertain us."

He hops to his feet. "I'll get the menus."

I laugh, getting up, too, and follow him downstairs.

Chapter Twenty-One

Dahlia

"To be clear," I groan, "this is not what I had in mind when I suggested you could find ways to entertain us tonight."

Either he misses the sarcasm altogether or he's a sadist who enjoys torturing me. Either way, his amusement at my displeasure from doing squats and lunges across the backyard for the last *eternity* is misplaced.

"You did great," he says.

"I never endeavored to be great at this. Being a mediocre lunger and squatter is something I can absolutely live with."

He holds the door open for me. "You should never accept mediocracy, especially in something that you hold the potential to excel in."

I stop in the foyer and smirk at him. "There's one time and one place that I care about my ability to squat. Fortunately for me, it's *your* stamina in that situation that's the weak link."

"Smart-ass."

I laugh, following him into the kitchen. "The pizza should be here any time. Think we have enough time to grab a shower?" I smack his ass as he walks in front of me. "If we shower simultaneously, it'll save time in the end."

"Has that ever worked for us?"

"Not once."

We laugh together, something I'm grateful for. I wasn't sure how we'd navigate our earlier tiff—he had every right to be angry—but we seemed to find a helpful way to communicate our way through it. I was glad he trusted me with his concerns about shouting. It made it easier to be genuine in my remorse, too.

I appreciate so many things about this man. But one of the biggest things I love about Troy falls into a category that none of the men I've dated before have ever scored in.

Effort.

He's surprised me with his ability and desire to show up for me—and not just in his protective hero role. I knew he was a loyal, dedicated man. But I can see he'll show up as my boyfriend, as a man, and as a friend. He'll show up as a person who wants to do more and better—to grow. That manifests itself in running the bath a little cooler than he'd like it because it's my preference or asking why I feel a certain way—not to pick a fight, but because he wants to understand my position. He's demonstrated it by standing with me when everyone else thought I was wrong or apologizing for his part in a disagreement with no reservation.

I smile at him.

"What?" he asks, handing me a bottle of water.

"I was just thinking about how things work out sometimes. One of the worst days of my life turned into the most beautiful thing in my life. It's funny how that happens."

"It's like it's fate or something."

"Do you believe in fate?" I ask, my stomach growling.

He takes a deep breath. "I don't know. I think people like to believe it when it serves them. Take us, for example. I want to think it's inevitable that we wound up together. It makes me hopeful that I can't fuck it up."

I kiss him quickly.

"What about you?" he asks.

"I didn't used to." I walk alongside him upstairs to our bathroom. "I thought that every day you made a series of choices that led you to another series of choices. And your choices were affected by other people's decisions. Like the world is a huge algorithm. But now? I don't know. I mean, we fit so well together that it's hard to imagine an opportunity for *us* not happening. You feel like the ..."

I blush, stopping myself short of finishing the sentence.

"Of what?"

"Nothing."

"No, of what?" He slips his shirt over his head, distracting me with his wide shoulders and cut abs. He tosses it on the bathroom vanity. "Finish it."

"You feel like the only thing in my life that was bound to happen. I know that sounds so corny."

He grins. "Up until a few days ago, I thought my life was a fucked-up and pointless series of events. I mean, what on earth could've been the purpose of going through some of the shit I have?" He shrugs. "But now, instead of feeling like a path of destruction, my life feels like a lane leading me right here."

"I'm so glad I give your path some structure."

He smirks, grabbing his half-hard cock through his sweats. "You give more than my path a little structure, Doll."

The humid air shifts, and I know where this leads. I start to undress to make the process easier when Troy's phone rings.

The levity on his face falls. My stomach churns. *It's time.*

"Ready for this?" he asks.

I force a swallow and nod because it's all I can do. I've fought thinking about this, and now it's here—Ford's meeting with my father.

Their conversation will either complicate or improve things.

While being in flux has been nerve-wracking, it's better than hearing Ford say he still suspects my dad is involved or that he's angry that we've questioned Alexis's potential role in this mess.

She is his wife, after all.

Troy answers on speakerphone.

"Castelli," he says, squeezing my shoulder.

"Hey. Is Dahlia there with you?"

"I'm here."

"Good. I just left your father's office."

"How did it go?" I ask, hoping my voice sounds calmer than I feel.

"He's a very interesting man. Not what I expected."

That doesn't answer my question, Ford. "That's lovely. How did it go?"

He chuckles. "He was very welcoming, much more than I would've expected from a man going through the legal battles he's currently embroiled in. We sat down over coffee, and I told him about the stalking and the emails. I stopped short of accusing Alexis. I just threw some crumbs down and watched to see how he dealt with them."

"Dammit, Ford. You're not getting points for storytelling here. Spit it out," I say.

He laughs. "Okay. He—"

Ding!

Troy bristles, his shoulders stiffening. "Hold up, Landry."

I glance out the window. There's a car parked in the driveway. I can see enough of the wording on the side to recognize the local pizza parlor we ordered from a while ago.

"It's just the pizza," I say. "Want me to get it?"

Troy looks over my shoulder toward the road. He nods warily. "Yeah. I already paid and tipped them. Grab the pizza and lock up behind you. Hang on, Landry." He swipes around on his phone. "There. The security system is off. I'll reset it as soon as you close the door."

Adriana Locke

"Thanks," I say, kissing his sternum before heading downstairs.

My nerves are jumbled. *What happened in Ford's meeting?* Saying he's a very interesting man isn't exactly helpful. *Is my father angry with me that he had to meet with my boss? Or will he appreciate they're not leaving any stone unturned?*

Does he have any answers?

I swing open the door. "Hey—*Oh my God.*"

* * *

Troy

"I'll wait until she's back to go into the details," Ford says. "But I have to admit one thing. Dahlia was right. He's much different in person than they portray him online."

"Does that surprise you?" I ask, pulling two towels out of the linen closet and putting them in Lincoln's bougie towel warmer. "When is the media ever right about someone? Claiming people are decent human beings doesn't sell subscriptions."

"You're so right. And they've made a pretty penny selling the story that Joseph Dallo is an asshole in bed with the cartel and planning on ruining humankind."

I laugh even though there's nothing funny about it. "So what's your gut reaction?"

"Oh, I have more than a gut reaction."

My ears perk up. "What does that mean? Do you know who's behind all of this?"

"Yes and no."

Fury greets me like an old friend. "Who the fuck is it?"

A car horn blows outside, which is an odd occurrence in this ritzy

180

neighborhood. It goes off again, this time followed by an engine revving and a crash.

"What is that? Hold on, Ford."

I peer out the window, curious but also ... unsettled.

Headlights sweep the shrubbery just before the pizza delivery car bolts down the driveway. The car jumps the curb, clipping the light pole at the bed where the driveway meets the road.

"What the fuck?"

"What's going on?" Ford asks, concern dripping in his tone.

I turn to find Dahlia but then notice one thing that sends waves of panic crashing through me.

Someone is in the passenger's seat with a bag over their head.

Chapter Twenty-Two

T roy

"*Fuck!*" My blood turns to ice as I race through the house. "Landry! Call Grey. Windsor Pizza delivery car just left Lincoln's. Will be headed to the causeway. Get him on this *now*."

He doesn't ask questions.

"*Dahlia!*"

I know she's not going to answer me.

I know she's not here.

* * *

Dahlia

"*You little fucking bitch.*" Freddy's voice is cold and detached but decidedly evil. "Why can't you ever fucking cooperate? *Huh?*"

I'm thrown back in the passenger's seat as the car barrels down the road. The engine screams, and the frame shakes. Freddy pushes it to its limit.

Tears stain my face, and snot drips into my mouth. I can't see anything through what I think is a pillowcase tied around my head.

Each ragged breath I take causes the fabric to pull into my mouth. *Stop, Dahlia. You won't be able to breathe. You need to stay alive. Keep your wits.*

But the lack of air is terrifying me, mixing with my pure, unadulterated fear.

What the hell is happening?

The side of my head throbs from Freddy smashing me in the face with what I'm guessing was his fist, ricocheting my skull off the window when I dove blindly for the horn.

Thank God, I hit it loud enough for Troy to hear it.

I know he did.

I believe he did.

"You couldn't just behave, could you?" Freddy asks from beside me. "I tried to help you, baby. I told you to take me back. I begged you not to do this. *I did.* I had it all planned out, and it could've been fine. It could've been great. But *you* had to ignore the rules of the game and tell people what was happening, and they started poking around in places they didn't need to be."

His voice grows louder and more frantic just before his fist connects with my head again.

"*Stop it!*" I scream. The pillowcase's nearly soaked and is clinging to my face. My chest heaves as I sob. "*Why are you doing this to me?*"

"This is all your fault. All of it. You cost me everything. *Everything*, dammit."

I have no idea what he's talking about. None of it makes sense. He's clearly unhinged.

I bring my hand to the side of my head, tapping it lightly against a warm goo near the top. A metallic odor floats through the air as my fingers touch what's undeniably blood soaking through the pillowcase.

"What's my fault?" I ask, the words barely audible around the fabric. *The wet material's going to suffocate me.*

The car quickly turns, and I smash into the door again.

I must get myself together. I have to survive.

I have to buy enough time for Troy to find me.

"You know Troy's coming for me," I say as calmly as I can manage. "You won't get away with this."

"What? Are you fucking him now too?"

"Are you looking over your shoulder? Because you should be."

His laugh is wicked. "The only thing behind me is the pizza delivery guy. But he's taking a little nap right now, so I think we'll be okay."

I still, my blood turning cold as I realize the horrifying truth ... *he's going to kill me.*

* * *

Troy

"I'm coming at you from the mainland," Grey says as soon as I answer his call. "What the hell's going on?"

I press the pedal to the floor, ripping by the guard shack at the neighborhood entrance. I can't see them before me, and catching up will be nearly impossible, considering their head start.

"Someone took Dahlia," I say, focusing on the task at hand and not on the fear gripping me like a vise. "They'll want to get off the island to avoid looping around. We have to catch them before they're off the causeway, or we could lose them in traffic."

"I'm ten minutes from you."

"*Fuck!*"

I scramble to remember the road layout on the island, which I memorized on the plane ride just a few days ago. A sign for the bike path entrance is up ahead. It's a nature road, if I remember correctly, and follows the shoreline. It's not made for cars, but ... "Fuck it."

Lincoln's car makes the sharp angle a breeze but doesn't love the terrain as much. Sand whips around us. It's replaced with water as I plow through a shallow wetland.

God help me. Help me get to her.

I force a swallow.

Please let me save her.

I can't lose the woman I'm utterly and completely in love with.

I can't.

I won't survive that.

Chapter Twenty-Three

D ahlia

"You can still walk away from this," I say, working to loosen the pillowcase as discreetly as I can. "You haven't done anything wrong that can't be forgiven." *Lies.* "I'll say I went with you, and we had things to work out." *More lies.* "This is just between you and me."

If I can get him to think he's not going to prison, he *might* reconsider this. *Maybe.* I have to give it a shot.

He laughs like a madman. *Or not.* "I've already killed the pizza delivery boy. He's a little involved, too."

My stomach hits the floor, my hands shaking. *No, Dahlia. Focus. Don't be a victim.*

I gather myself. "Well, that's one death," I say as casually as possible. "And maybe you'll kill me. But I promise you, Freddy, Troy *will* find you. And when he does, you'll wish you hadn't done this. Think about that."

Tears lick my eyes because I know I'm right. Troy will not sleep until he finds him. *Until he finds me.*

I've thought about his words earlier ... "*I just want to protect you and make you happy. And I worry I can't do that. I worry I can't do that. I worry I can't keep you safe, and you'll see that I'm a fraud.*"

Those words were the most vulnerable thing I've ever heard from him. They say everything.

They say he loves me.

My shoulders shake as I struggle not to cry. If something happens to me, if I don't figure a way out, it will devastate him.

I can't be the thing that ruins him.

"Don't say that," Freddy says.

"I'm trying to help you."

"I said *shut the fuck up.*"

I free the edge of the fabric and gulp blood-scented air. My stomach clenches. *I might puke.*

"What do you want?" I ask. *Keep him talking.* I heard Ford say that once. Keep them talking to humanize yourself. "Why are you doing this? You obviously want something, so let me help you get it."

"See, that's the thing, baby. You are helping me get it."

"How?"

He swerves again, smashing me against the door. I wince as pain rockets through my head.

I consider finding the handle and jumping out. I could probably pull that off. *But if I do, where am I? Will I get run over or fall into a swamp? Will I break every bone in my body?*

Stay calm. Wait for Troy.

"Remember when you took me to your daddy's house for dinner, and we met your stepmommy?" he asks.

Alexis. "Yes."

"Turns out your stepmommy has a sweet little cunt on her. She's insatiable. Unlike you. *Frigid bitch.* You got that from your dad, it seems. Neither of you want to fuck enough."

Focus, Dahlia. "Interesting observation."

"But then she found out she's gonna be a widow sooner than later, and she didn't want to risk losing that. Sorry about that, by the way. Even your daddy doesn't want you until he knows he has an exit strategy."

What?

"You know about the cancer, right? Stage three. Bone." He groans, hitting the gas. "Guess he started fearing the afterlife and figured he better make good with you in case God is real."

He's lying. He must be. I would've known that.

"Yeah, I knew about that," I lie. "Thanks for your sympathy."

"The fucker really messed up my plans. Now Alexis thinks there's nothing I can do for her. What does she need little ole me for?" He pats my thigh, the contact making me shudder. "You. You're what I can do for her."

I close my eyes and grip the door. "Why me?"

"If I get rid of you, she gets the whole inheritance. Which, rightfully, she deserves. She's been fucking him for that money for longer than he's known you. You're a grave robber really."

What the hell is happening here?

"But what good is all that money to you if you're dead?" I ask. "Surely, you've thought about that."

His laughter cuts through me. It's wild. Maniacal. *Unholy.*

"I hate to break it to you, baby, but I'm looking in the rearview right now, and your boy isn't coming for—*shit!*"

* * *

Troy

The front of my car crashes into the pizza delivery car, spinning it like a top. Glass breaks, spilling onto the road. Tires squeal. The smell of rubber and exhaust fills the air as the car with Dahlia goes careening into a marsh.

I jump out of my car and around the front. The engine smokes, and fluids sizzle against the hot metal. I run to the other car, submerged in just a few feet of water, and immediately search for Dahlia.

My heart breaks as she pulls a pillowcase off her head.

She's dazed. Bleeding. And sitting next to a madman.

A madman who's about to die.

Freddy kicks his door frantically, but it's jammed. I hop on the car's hood and slide over it, kicking Freddy in the face as he exits.

He falls to the side, splashing into the water, a piece of metal catching the light in his hand.

"He has a gun!" Dahlia screams from inside the car.

It's a relief to hear her voice, but I can't even look at her.

Neutralize the threat.

And this motherfucker's going to pay.

I draw my gun as Freddy gets to his feet. He dives toward the car as Dahlia exits, then grabs her by the front of her hair—yanking a handful so hard her face bounces off the door. She screams as he stands her up just as I'm coming around the door.

He stops me in my tracks ... by shoving the gun into the side of her skull.

Dahlia's eyes are wild—wide and full of fear. Tears flow down her cheeks, mixing with what's unmistakably blood.

Fuck. She whimpers, pulling away from the gun.

Don't blink. Stay calm, Castelli.

"Let me walk out of here, or I'm killing the bitch," Freddy says, yanking her arm.

Dahlia cries, and her body shakes. But she's alert and aware.

She hasn't given up. *That's it, Doll. Stay with me.*

I assess the situation quickly. If he's going to kill her, he's going to kill her either way. So I take a steadying breath and try to play chess with a child.

"I *will* kill this bitch!" he yells again, the gun trembling in his hand.

"Well, that'll be two dead bitches today. The choice is yours."

"I'll shoot her in the face. Do you want to see that? Do you want to see her blood in the water and know you didn't save her?"

My chest tightens.

"Mom! Hold on! Trav is calling an ambulance!"

Everything's red. The floor. Her shirt. My hands.

She looks up at me and tries to smile.

"Can't ..." she whispers, the words gurgling in her throat.

"Mom!" I yell, ripping my shirt off and trying to stop the blood from pouring out of her skull. "Mom, hang in there. Please."

"Can't save me, Troy. You can't ..."

Her eyes flutter closed. Her lifeless body relaxes peacefully in my lap as I scream.

My jaw flexes. *No. Stay. Fucking. Focused.* "Do you want to know what I think?"

"What's that?" he asks.

"I think you're going to kill her anyway. If I let you walk out of here, she's dead. And if I don't ... she's dead."

Dahlia cries out, but I ignore it. *I have to.* I have to get that gun out of his hand.

"So I have a choice to make," I say, buying time. "Do I let you kill her here or somewhere else? That's a pretty easy choice."

He jerks her closer to him. The sight of him touching her makes me sick.

"I'm going to do you a favor," I say, moving slowly toward them. "I'm going to let you see what it feels like to settle something like a man. You've probably never done that before, have you?"

He backs away, confused. His grip on the gun loosens as he tries to wrap his head around what I'm doing.

"It's better this way," I say, keeping his attention on me. "If you kill her somewhere else, I'll have to expend a lot of energy to find you. That's just extra locations and more time. Let's keep it simple."

"What the fuck are you talking about?" he asks.

I lift my gun in front of me, barrel to the water, and drop it unceremoniously. Dahlia cries out again.

Trust me, Doll.

"Let's settle this here," I say, edging closer. "Man to man. Hell, you can even keep your gun. That'll even out the odds a little. You're obviously feeling yourself today. Your chances are probably as good as they're gonna get."

"What the fuck is wrong with you?" he asks, the gun wobbling.

I leap forward and knock the gun out of his hand. Dahlia screams, her voice piercing the marsh, and Freddy reaches for the gun.

I grab his head by the hair and dunk it underwater. He flails—arms going wild, clawing at me—scrambling to reach any part of me he can.

Fury takes over as I yank him back up. He takes a gulp of air.

"Get a big breath. Don't pass out yet." I smack the side of his face. "Stick with me, big boy."

He gasps just before I sling him underwater once again.

"*Oh my God*," Dahlia cries, huddled by the car.

I knee him in the face once, twice, three times. With every hit, he gets weaker.

"Come on, Freddy," I say, seething. "Back up you go."

He sputters, sucking air and trying to scramble away.

My fist cracks his jaw. I can feel the bones crumble as I rip the punch through his face.

He gasps, his mouth hanging open, as he takes a punch on the other side of his jaw.

"*Fuck you*," I say, hauling him to dry land by the front of his shirt. "You're nothing but a piece of fucking shit."

I deposit him on the ground in a lump.

"You were killing bitches today, remember?" I kick him in the ribs. "Where'd that badass go?"

He moans, lying in a lump on the sandy ground.

I straddle him, gripping him again by his tattered shirt. My face is inches from his. "You won't ever fuck with her again, will you? *Will you?*"

He's unable to move his mouth.

I palm his forehead and move his head up and down.

"There you go," I say, tossing him away like the garbage that he is. "I'm glad we're on the same page."

"Castelli!" Grey runs down the hill. "You okay?"

I spit the taste of the marsh out of my mouth. "I'm fine." I look over my shoulder. "Need to check my girl. Make sure he stays put."

Grey looks down and sighs. "The only way he's going anywhere is on a stretcher or with a pair of wings, my friend."

Sirens wail in the distance as I race back to the car.

Dahlia runs to me, leaping into my arms. Her head buries in the crook of my neck as she sobs.

"Are you okay?" I ask, trying to inspect her. She won't let go enough for me to see. "Hey, are you okay? Where's this blood coming from?"

She pulls back. Her eyes are fucking swollen and black. Tears mix with blood on her cheeks.

The taste of vomit coats my tongue. I hold her precious face in my hands and inspect the gash at her temple and the swelling and blood on the other side of her head.

"I think my arm is broken," she says, her right arm dangling at her side.

"My God. Doll. *I'm so sorry.*"

The sirens grow louder as I hold her close to me, careful not to touch her injuries. I close my eyes, saying a prayer.

"You saved me, Troy," she whispers in my ear. "I knew you would."

I press a kiss on her head as the medics arrive. "I'd do anything for you."

"I know."

Her words settle into my psyche—her confidence in me. Her faith. *Her love.*

I may not be enough for Dahlia—she deserves the world—but no one will love her as much as me.

And that just might be enough.

Chapter Twenty-Four

Dahlia

"Are you feeling okay?" Troy asks from beside me.

"Yeah. I feel like I was kidnapped and was then in a car accident. You know, just another day."

My antics are not entertaining him. The sour look on his face makes me laugh.

"I have to laugh about this, Troy. If not, a deep, dark hole is waiting to crush me. Oh, speaking of crashes, if I weren't the one being thrown into the door with a maniac with a gun sitting beside me and a pizza guy in the trunk, that would've been really hot."

He groans, looking at the ceiling of Jason Brewer's plane.

"I can't imagine what your forearms looked like controlling the car like that," I say, licking my bottom lip. "And the way your face gets all linear when you're focused. Maybe when I'm better, we can figure out how to replicate that without the broken humerus and concussion and various lacerations."

"You're going to pay for this."

"I'm looking forward to it."

He looks at me through the corner of his eye and tries not to smile.

I rest my head on his non-broken humerus and yawn.

Thanks to the Landry connections, doctors saw me right away. I'm going to live, which I knew as soon as I saw Troy climb out of the car, although with a little less blood and a lot more inflammation.

"We need to make sure we send a sizable tip to the pizza guy when we get home," I say. "Freddy told me he killed him. He really thought he was dead."

"Already took care of it."

I flinch. "You did?"

"Yeah, since the bastards wouldn't let me go back with you for all the tests, I had time to process every fucking minute of that ordeal. Becca's getting the contact information so I can take care of it this week."

I lift my head and look at him curiously. "Becca, huh?"

He smirks.

I'm just screwing with him—he knows that. Becca is the sweetest person I've ever met, and Troy almost killed a man for me.

Lights twinkle on the ground below as we sail quietly through the night sky. Everything's a bit *more* tonight. The stars are prettier. The cookies the stewardess served us when we got on board were sweeter. The guy next to me is more irresistible.

"What are you thinking about?" he asks, stretching his legs out in front of him.

"Just that when we land, things will be different. There's so much to figure out and navigate."

"Like what?"

"How do I work with a broken arm? Will Ford even let me work after I broke protocol and answered the phone, which caused this whole damn thing? I'm also screwing my co-worker, and that's probably against the handbook."

He exhales. "Freddy didn't track your phone. He had a tracker in your bag. He knew where we were the whole time."

"*What?* Are you serious?" The thought of him watching us, sneaking around, preying on us for those days makes me ill. "How do you know?"

"People say things when they're under duress."

"Did you find it?"

"Grey did. It's tech that's not mainstream yet. It's still in beta. I don't know how in the hell he got it, but he did." He pulls his phone out and opens his camera reel. "Here. I saved this for you while you were getting your X-ray."

I take his phone and look at the picture.

Breaking News: All charges against Dallo dropped by prosecution.

I gasp. "What?"

"That's what Ford was calling to tell us. Or a part of it, anyway." He takes his phone and slips it back in his pocket. "The forensic accounting firm discovered money laundering and other things happening with Dallo Metalworks. But a few months ago, they arrested a bunch of cartel guys in Atlanta and got some of them to turn state's evidence." Troy yawns. "Turns out that your grandfather really was a bad apple, and two of his seeds were still working for your father. The CFO and CIO, I think. Your dad cooperated with them for weeks and helped them build their case. It's a tangled web."

My heart warms, either from the pain medication or because my father isn't a con man. Maybe both.

"They got indicted last night," he says, furrowing his brows. "Or tonight. Hell, I don't know what time it is. We were in the marsh, and they were getting indicted."

"Does my father know about Alexis?"

"I'm going to let the two of you have that conversation. Short answer is yes. But that's all I'm saying."

I shrink against the seat.

Although I'm not close with my father, hearing that I'm probably going to lose him stings more than I anticipated. Like he said, I'd hoped we could figure things out and maybe have a real relationship. But everyone has choices. I don't know why I expected his to be different.

"What's that about?" he asks.

"Nothing."

He winks. "Don't draw any conclusions from what I said. Keep that sunny optimism you annoy me with," he says, teasing me.

I roll my eyes.

"I do have a problem I want to discuss with you." Troy clears his throat and sits up. "Might as well do it now."

"You don't get to be mean to me. If you have bad news or think we need some space, you're wrong. I do not agree. And if you think I'm a fool now because of the phone thing, even though that *actually* didn't cause any problems ... you'll be right."

He smiles.

"If it's an employment situation, I can't work anyway," I say, looking at my arm that needs a cast tomorrow morning. "I'll quit. You don't get Becca, but I'll quit and work at a bakery. I'd be good at a bakery."

He starts to laugh.

"I'm not laughing," I say. "You're stuck with me, Castelli. I learned stalking tips thanks to this unfortunate incident. I will stalk you. You're mine."

His smile softens, and his head cocks to the side. "Say that again."

"You're mine." I blush under his gaze. "You're mine even though you force me to lift weights and get sugar and cinnamon all over the counter in the mornings when you make toast. And you can't get a stain out for shit. You ruined that white shirt with spaghetti sauce."

He shakes his head, amused.

"And you can be *super bossy*," I point out. "I hate to bring this up, but your driving could use some work. You can't park a truck, and then you spin the pizza car so that I hit the door when you could've hit it the other way and slung me into the center. I wouldn't have a broken humerus."

"Will you shut up?"

"I'm just pointing out all the things that most women may not like. But me? I like them. I like you just the way you are. Remember that if you want to go fuck around."

"Don't you think it's too soon to joke about all of this?"

I try hard not to smile. "I'm not joking. My arm hurts."

He carefully grabs my face and brings me in for a kiss. It's soft and sweet—the most tender kiss he's ever given me.

And I just found a new reason to love Troy Castelli.

"I'm glad you're not joking," he says, sitting back. "Because what I was going to say before your inane monologue was that I don't think I can sleep without you. And I'm probably going to be *slightly* over-protective for a while. You can't use your humerus, as you keep pointing out. You might need help."

"What's your point?" I ask, my spirits rising.

"We should live together. And if you're thinking it's too fast for that, then just for a little while. I just …" He sighs. "I love you."

The bridge of my nose burns like it does before I cry. I start to climb onto his lap, but my seat belt and the searing pain in my arm stop me.

"Sit still," he says. "We're getting ready to land."

I turn as much as I can to face him. "Since I'm so totally in love with you, I'm glad you want to live together. I was thinking—"

He swallows the rest of the words with a kiss—one that doesn't stop until the pilot asks us to please leave the plane.

Chapter Twenty-Five

Dahlia

"That ain't necessary," Burt grumbles. "I'm not doing it. I don't care how many times you ask."

Burt sits in his recliner, eating a piece of chocolate cake I brought him from Hillary's House. He's unshaven, and his hair's a mess. But his eyes are bright, and he's still a piece of work, so I think he'll be all right.

"But Burt ..." I say, sticking out my bottom lip.

He scoffs. "Don't come in here pouting with your little lip hanging out, your broken arm, and busted head. I had broken ribs and almost lost my spleen. I get the sympathy."

Troy leans against the wall and watches Burt and I argue about him moving across town to be near us. We decided living at Troy's was easier once the sun came up. Bigger house. *Nicer house.* Closer to work, assuming we still have jobs.

And no bad memories.

"You're going to cost me a lot of time," I say. "I hope you know that."

"I've never asked you for nothing. If you waste your time, it ain't because of me."

"Damn you, Burt."

"*Damn you, Burt*," he says, mocking me. "I'm grouchy, all right. I'm ..." He glances at the clock. "Fifteen minutes until I can get more pain meds."

I stand, the red couch squeaking, and sigh.

Someone knocks on the door. Troy silently asks if he can answer it and Burt waves his hand in agreement.

"Hey," Morgan says, bounding into the room. "That hottie next door said you were here. How are you feeling?" She looks around me. "Hey, Burtie."

"Hey, babe."

I stifle a laugh. Morgan's eyes twinkle with mischief.

"How are you?" she asks me again.

"Fine. In some pain but, I mean, it probably just comes with the territory."

"You're really moving in with Troy?"

"Yes, she is. Don't try to talk her out of it," he says from across the room.

She looks at him and laughs. "I'm Morgan. I'm the best friend, not to be confused with Burt, the *best neighbor*. I'd love to have coffee with you this week so I can ensure you understand how much I love this girl, and if you ever hurt her, I will hurt you. Worse than you hurt Freddy."

"Fuck Freddy," Burt says.

"I'm assuming the man, and I do mean *man*, in Dahlia's house is your brother because those genes are strong."

"Yeah. That's Travis," Troy says.

"Well, Troy, since you and I are friends now, how about introducing me? I'm a catch."

"She is," Burt says, rocking in his chair. "Gives good sponge baths, too."

Morgan and I laugh.

"Okay, since you're alive and well ..." She looks at Troy and then back at me. "And in what appears to be very capable hands, I'm going back to your house to flirt with Troy's brother."

"We need to go, too," I say.

Morgan gasps. "At least give me ten minutes alone with him. *Damn.* Don't cockblock me."

She gives us no time to respond. She's out the door as quickly as she came in.

I go to Burt's chair and kneel beside it. He pats my hand and frowns.

"I'm sorry to see you go, sweet pea," he says.

"I'm not gone yet."

Troy makes a face that only I can see. I roll my eyes at him.

"We're just getting the basic stuff today since we aren't working," I say. "It'll be a couple of weeks before I'm completely out. But then I'm just a call away. And you better believe I'll be here to celebrate all kinds of things. Like sunny days and that I got up in the morning, and we'll have two pieces of cake when Troy makes me lift weights."

Troy shakes his head, resolved to my hatred of weightlifting.

Burt shifts in his chair. "I'm sad to see you go, but I'm proud of you. I didn't have any kids, thank God, but if I had, I'd hope I'd have a girl like you."

"Damn you, Burt," I say, sniffling.

He chuckles. "Come and see me." He points at Troy. "You, too. I want to make sure you kids are all right."

I stand, squeezing his wrinkled hand. "I'm sorry again for—"

"Get her outta here, will ya?" Burt asks Troy.

Troy shakes Burt's hand. "It was nice meeting you."

"You, too." Burt nods at him. "Happy to finally see her with someone worthy of her. Take care of her. She's my *best neighbor*."

"I will. Don't worry about that."

Burt winks at me, then turns on his television.

Troy holds my hand as we leave.

We step onto the sidewalk beneath one of the massive trees lining the street. Our steps are slow and unrushed. It's a nice change of pace from the past few days.

"Who's that?" Troy asks, nodding to a dark-colored SUV crawling up the street. He shifts his body so he's between me and the SUV.

It rolls in front of my house and stops. My father steps out of the driver's side door.

My heart pounds. I have no idea why he's here. I haven't talked to him since before I left town. After everything that's happened, I'm not sure what he'll say.

"Hi, Dahlia. Hello, Troy," he says.

"How do you two know each other?" I ask.

My dad smiles. "We had a long chat last night."

Is that so?

I look curiously at Troy. He doesn't look at me.

Troy kisses my cheek. "If you're okay, I'm going to make sure your friend hasn't hog-tied my brother."

I laugh. "That's a good plan."

"Nice to see you, Mr. Dallo," Troy says.

"Likewise."

They shake hands before Troy walks off.

"How are you feeling?" he asks me.

"Just like you'd expect, only with pain meds."

He nods, exhaling roughly. "Well, this isn't how I thought we'd have this conversation someday. And it's not the exact conversation I thought we'd have, either."

"Wanna take a walk?" I ask.

He smiles. "I'd love to."

We stroll through the neighborhood in silence. I don't know what to say, and basic pleasantries feel wrong. We pass three houses before he speaks.

"I'm getting a divorce," he says.

"Wow. Strong lead."

He chuckles. "I believe Alexis didn't know that Freddy would go after you. Maybe she did. I'm not defending her. She's certainly not innocent. She was having an affair with your boyfriend, of all people. And she made it very clear, both to others and to me last night when I confronted her about it, that she has major problems that I have a daughter."

"I hate that. I want to apologize, but I didn't ask to be born, you know?"

"I don't want you to apologize. You're the best thing that ever came from me."

My gaze falls to the ground.

"I knew she didn't love me when I married her," he continues. "I'm not that self-absorbed to know that a woman like Alexis generally doesn't fall in love with a man like me."

"Did you love her?"

He shakes his head and shrugs. "No. I cared about her, yes. But I didn't love her."

"Then why did you marry her, if you don't mind me asking?"

He kicks a rock into the gutter. "I didn't get married to Alexis because I always hoped your mother would have a change of heart. I'm not blaming her for what happened. I was as adamant, maybe more, that you weren't raised in the same world I grew up in. But a part of me secretly hoped that magic would happen and there would be a chance for us to be together." He looks at me and smiles. "She was the great love of my life."

I can't stop the tears. I don't even try.

"She was alone her entire life, and I think it was because she wanted to be with you," I say. "It hurts me so much to know she died without ever feeling loved. You know?"

"Life is unfair. It can be so ugly and painful. Penelope's and my love was impossible. But the thing that would make both of us happy, and I do feel I can take the liberty to speak for her about this, is to see you find love. To see you happy."

I sniffle, wiping my nose with the end of my shirt.

"I could've overlooked Alexis's unfaithfulness," he says. "I can overlook a lot. But she asked me to pick between you, and I picked you."

My gaze snaps to his.

"I hope that we can have a father-daughter relationship someday. I want to be a part of your life and you to be a part of mine. I want to know what kind of card to get you for your birthday and have a stocking in my house with your name on it. You'll have kids that I want to know and love ... if you'll allow me the privilege."

We stop and face each other, and I look at him differently. For the first time, I see a man who could be my dad and not just my father.

"I'd like that a lot, too."

"Great."

We walk around the block, talking about all sorts of things—our first cars, my job, what he sees in the future for Dallo Metalworks. I found a way to ask him if he had cancer, like Freddy said. It turns out that Freddy was full of shit. Turns out that Freddy *was* responsible for everything done to me. And it sickens me to know that. It wasn't a prank, though. He was truly a sick and twisted bastard.

Our conversation flows easily, naturally, and by the time we return to my house, I feel like a weight has been lifted from me.

Troy stands on the porch, waiting for me. "Our helpers just left to get brunch."

"Brunch, huh?"

He chuckles and shrugs.

"I'm going to let you both go," my father says, shaking Troy's hand again. "Take care of my daughter, and I'll see you Saturday?"

"Let me run it by Dahlia first, then I'll let you know."

My father hugs me gently, careful to avoid my injuries. "If you need anything, call me. You are my priority. I can't fix my mistakes, but I can try not to make any more."

"That's all any of us can do."

"I'll see you." He waves and heads to his car.

"Hey!" I call after him as Troy slips an arm around my waist.

My father looks at me, his hand on the door.

"Thanks, Dad."

He nods, his face wrinkling, and ducks in the car. We watch him drive away.

"What's Saturday?" I ask as we return to my house.

"He wants to go golfing."

"You golf? With your temper?"

He chuckles, shutting the door behind us. "I don't love it. But when you're with the Landrys, it's a skill you somehow acquire."

I busy myself packing up some of my things in the kitchen. Troy packs up my books in the living room. I love that he didn't question that I needed them to go first.

I think through everything that has happened over the past week and how much my life has changed. It could've gone so horribly. I could've lost everything—even my life.

Things can change so fast. In the blink of an eye, in a heartbeat, things can go one way or the other. How much time did I waste on mediocre boyfriends? Mom and my dad wasted their whole lives hoping something would happen and they could be together. Alexis wasted the past three years trying to con her way into an inheritance.

I watch the man I love pack my romance books in totes. My very own hero.

I don't want to wait to have the life I want. I want to live it now ... with him.

"Hey," I say.

He looks up. "Yeah?"

"I'm just letting you know that I want to have your baby."

He drops a stack of books into the tote. "What are you telling me?"

"*That I want to have your baby.* I want to point at you across the soccer field and tell the other moms that you're my baby's daddy. I want to see you standing in the middle of the night feeding our daughter. And I want to watch you teach our son ... not to drive. I'll do that."

He bursts out laughing.

"We didn't have that childhood, but we can have that life together. That's the life I want ... with you. So what are we waiting for?"

He walks toward me, unbuttoning his shirt. "I'm not."

I laugh as the door opens, and Morgan and Travis walk in. Troy's face falls, and I laugh harder.

"Did we interrupt something?" Travis asks, looking between us.

Troy and I look at each other and smile.

"We have time," I say softly.

He glances at the clock. "Fifteen minutes."

"I meant the rest of our life."

He turns to his brother and my friend. "You have fourteen minutes. Then we're gone."

My house is full of voices, laughter, and people I love. I already know I'll love Travis. I loved him before I met him.

Troy pulls me into him, kissing the top of my head. "Have I told you lately that I love you?"

"It's been probably twenty minutes."

He chuckles. "I never thought I'd tell another person I love them, and I can't tell you enough."

"I love you right back."

Epilogue

T roy

Two weeks later ...

"I'm over here." Lincoln Landry leans against the doorway of the break room with a shit-eating grin on his face. "Just in case you didn't see me."

"Like I ask you every time you're here. Why?"

"Very funny." He follows me to my office like a puppy. "I don't even get a *thank you?*"

I hold the door open for him like the diva he is and then close it. He gets entirely too comfortable in the chair across from me.

"I believe I told you thank you for letting us use your house," I say. "But *thank you* again."

"What about the rest of it?"

I have no idea what he's talking about.

"Linc, today is my first day back. It's early." *I'd rather be home with my girl.* "Very early. I wouldn't say I like these guessing games in the afternoon. I sure as hell don't like them before the sun is up."

207

"The bed!"

I flinch. "What?"

"Dude, I literally had every bedroom in that house cleared out except one. My guys did it within a two-hour window. Danielle doesn't know this, so hopefully, I can get it all put back the way she had it before we go down there in a couple of weeks." He cringes. "But I hooked you up."

Oh, for fuck's sake.

"That's why there was one bed in the house?" I ask.

"Yup. I was helping you make some moves. The two of you have danced around each other for two years. If it didn't work out, the couch is pretty nice."

"You know what? I hate to say it, but you might've had a hand in this. So all sarcasm aside, *thank you.*"

"Did you just say thank you to Lincoln?" Ford grimaces, coming in with a cup of coffee. "Also, why are you here, Linc?"

"I said the same thing."

"Good to have you back, Troy. How's Dahlia?"

"She's here, actually. She said she can't sit at home doing nothing."

"I told her to take time off. What is it with you two?" Ford asks.

I shrug.

He swipes his phone screen. It rings through the speaker.

"Hi, Ford," Dahlia says.

I furrow a brow.

"Good morning. I'm in Troy's office. Could you come by, please?"

"Sure. Be right there."

It's not thirty seconds before there's a knock on my door.

"Come in," I say.

She enters with a confused look on her face.

I helped her get dressed this morning—black pants and a loose-fitting top. Her arm has been hurting, and she didn't sleep well. So I sat up reading to her, trying to keep her mind off the pain.

"What's going on?" she asks, looking around the room.

"How do you feel?" Ford asks.

"It hurts. A lot."

Ford kicks back, resting one ankle on the other knee. "I have a proposition for the two of you."

Dahlia comes around my desk and stands beside me.

"Okay," I say, wondering where this is going.

"I'm in a bit of a pickle with the two of you. I don't love the idea of Troy being in the field and Dahlia in the office."

"So you want me in the field. Makes sense," Dahlia says with a nod.

I snort.

Ford laughs. "Not where I was going, but interesting angle." He shakes his head. "Maybe you'd like to head our new Safety and Consulting division. We've been thinking about it for a long time. Troy, I think we've talked about it before."

"Yeah. We sure have."

"You can totally say no," Ford says. "We'll figure it out. But I'd like to dip our toes into consulting, and I don't have anyone else I'd trust to run it. It might be a perfect fit."

Dahlia looks at me.

"Wow," I say. "That's a big deal. Are you sure?"

"You're my best guy. Don't tell Theo. It'll hurt his feelings."

"I'm definitely telling Theo."

Lincoln and Dahlia laugh.

"But, seriously, yes. I think it's a great idea. Thank you, Ford."

"Why don't you two come into my office in a couple of hours? I have a few things to take care of, and then we'll discuss specifics. Get a game plan together."

"We'll be there," Dahlia says, resting her hand on my shoulder.

Ford turns to her and smiles. "I'm going to add a new section in our protocol handbook that says always trust a woman's intuition." He points at her. "I should've listened to you about Freddy. I'm sorry."

"I appreciate the apology. I'm also sorry for dragging you all through that."

"Like I said, you're family." Ford motions for Lincoln to follow him. "Come on, Lincoln. Leave my employees alone. Why *are* you here, anyway?"

They close the door behind them.

"You know," Dahlia says, standing in front of me. "We could do some serious role-playing here. I could be your naughty secretary, and you could be my big, bad boss."

I grab her ass and bring her closer. "Keep it up, and your boss will order you to go home."

"Why? Because I think you're hot?"

"No. Because you're going to make me want to fuck you so bad that I'll have to take you home so the whole office doesn't hear you scream."

She groans. "I'm so wet right now."

I look up at her, into her beautiful eyes, and only see love. There's no judgment or disappointment, no fear or apathy. Only the same way I feel about her reflected back to me.

"We can have that life together. That's the life I want ... with you. So what are we waiting for?"

I've considered her words countless times, wondering if it's too fast. *Will she regret it at some point? Is this the honeymoon phase where it's all sunshine and roses?* Except there was a car chase, an assault or two, and a stalker.

But it's not. Her love is consistent. And I know I'll never stop loving this woman.

I remember the last time my morning started like this, with Ford and Lincoln in my office. And the only piece of advice that Lincoln has ever shared with me—even if it doesn't entirely make sense—stuck.

"You don't need a parachute to skydive. You only need a parachute to skydive twice."

I take a deep breath ... and jump.

"Will you marry me?" I ask.

Dahlia's jaw drops. "Are you serious?"

"I'm ill-prepared. I don't have a ring or a speech or a pretty location. But I'm jumping."

"Jumping?"

I laugh. "I'm asking you to marry me anyway. We'll buy you whatever ring you want. I want you, and I want you to know I'm always here for you. Every day. For the rest of my life."

She cups my chin in the one hand she can lift and grins. "I'd love nothing more than to be Mrs. Castelli."

"Want to sneak out of here for a couple of hours?"

"I thought you'd never ask."

The End

Keep reading for Chapter One of Adriana's bestselling novel, The Proposal ...

The Proposal

Synopsis

Breaking News: Rugby's bad boy marries his best friend's little sister

If Renn Brewer would've asked me to marry him, I would've said no.

Why?

One, his reputation precedes him. His name is in the headlines at least once a month. Two, he's not just my brother's best friend. *They're teammates.* And three, I'm in my self-care era.

Unfortunately, a version of me equates self-care with bad choices.

The cocktail in my hand—similar to the one that got me into this situation—is the prettiest shade of pink. It's almost the same color as the giant rock on my left hand. And instead of discussing an annulment,

The Proposal

I'm considering a 90-day marriage of convenience to the man I accidentally married in Las Vegas.

Renn didn't propose marriage. But he does deliver a proposal I might be unable to turn down.

USA Today and Amazon Charts Bestselling author Adriana Locke delivers a **"spicy & sweet!" forbidden sports romance with a marriage of convenience** that will make you swoon!

Chapter One
Blakely

"Could you die quietly?" Ella sighs, pulling her sunglasses down and squinting into the sunlight. "And maybe do it over there, please?"

Two quintessential frat boys, a label I'd bet my life on yet feels like a disservice to fraternities everywhere, cease their constant complaints about being hungover. Their whining is a show, a pathetic effort to gain attention, and one we're over—especially Ella.

They fire a dirty look at my best friend. She cocks a brow, challenging them right back, and waits.

Lying on the chaise next to her, I smirk. *How many seconds will it take for them to realize they're outgunned by a five-foot-three pistol with bubble-gum pink toenails?*

Eight ... Nine ... Ten ...

They gather their things quietly, watching Ella like she might toss them into the pool if they don't act quickly enough.

I wouldn't be shocked if that happened, either.

Ella St. James doesn't surprise me much anymore. She carried a tray of freshly baked snickerdoodle cookies when she rang my doorbell three years ago. She was adorable, wearing an apron with embroidered cherries and a white silk ribbon in her hair while welcoming me to the Nashville neighborhood. It starkly contrasted with the following weekend when she took me out so I could *get acquainted with the city*. That night ended with Ella jacking some guy's jaw for trying to grope me on the dance floor and me picking her up from the police station in an Uber at three in the morning.

"Thank you," she says, sliding the glasses up her nose and returning to her book.

Las Vegas is sweltering. Blue water sparkles just inches from our feet, and I swear it only amplifies the sun's rays. We should probably get a massage or go shopping to beat the unbearable heat, but I didn't fly for almost four hours to stay inside.

I could've celebrated my new job and birthday like that in Tennessee.

"How do you think I would look with red hair?" I ask, stretching my legs in front of me. "Not bright cherry red, but a more purple-y, crimson-y red."

"No."

I furrow my brows. "That wasn't a yes or no question."

"I was cutting to the chase." Her fingertip trails along the bottom of the paperback. "That's not the question you were really asking."

It wasn't? I settle against my chair. *Yeah, it wasn't.*

It was a last-minute attempt at being young and reckless before I turn thirty tomorrow.

This whole birthday crap has been a bit of a mind fuck.

I've lived the past ten years with little abandon. I've traveled, dated, and swam with sharks. Went on a ten-city tour with a rock band. Attended a movie premiere, got engaged (and unengaged), and ate pizza at the world's oldest pizzeria in Naples. *Check that off the bucket list.* And with every year of fun, I assumed I had nothing to worry about—that I would have my shit together before I turned thirty and became a real adult.

That was an incorrect assumption.

By all accounts, I should be in a stable relationship and burdened with a mortgage and enough debt to bury my soul until Jesus returns.

Appliances should excite me. I should have a baby. *I should understand life insurance.* Instead, I just broke up with *another* bad boy with commitment issues, re-upped the rental contract on my townhouse, and refilled my birth control.

But that all ends in six hours. I have to turn over a new leaf when the sun comes up. It's time.

Ella's book snaps closed. "This is not a tri-life crisis, Blakely. It's just a birthday."

"I know that."

"But do you?"

"*Yes, I do,*" I say, mocking her. "I'm not in crisis mode. I'm just transitioning into this new era of buying eye cream and freezing my eggs, and it's a little ... terrifying."

She sighs. "You've been buying eye cream for years."

"Yeah, as a hedge against the future. This *is* the future."

Ella rolls onto her side, brushing her dark hair off her shoulder. "While I can't relate because I have a solid two years before I'm thirty—"

"Was that necessary?"

She laughs. "You're freaking out for no reason. Tomorrow is just another day."

"I know. *I really do.* There's just this pressure to get my ducks in a row and start making serious progress, or else I'll be fifty with no husband or kids. And I want both."

"All I ask is that you be a little more selective on the husband part because the last few guys you've dated ..." She whistles. "Not good, Blakely."

Yeah, I know.

"I know you feel your biological clock ticking or whatever it is, but you *have* been doing big things," she says. "You're the new artist manager assistant at Mason Music Label. Remember, you little badass? That's impressive."

I shrug happily at the reminder. That's true—a dream come true, really. *And even more of a reason to get my shit together.* "But would I be even more impressive as a redhead?"

"The answer is still no."

I groan. "*Come on.* I want to go out on something big. Something fun. Something wild that I'll remember while I'm taking vitamins and going to bed before ten."

Ella reaches for her water. "Fine. But let's find something else. Red doesn't suit your skin tone."

"Like what? I'm not getting anything pierced, and I don't think I'm ready to commit to a tattoo."

"You've been wanting a tattoo since the day I met you. As a matter of fact, weren't you looking at tattoos when I brought over those cookies?"

I laugh. "Yes. But it's so permanent. What if I don't want it next week?"

She rolls her eyes.

"What else is there?" I ask. "Let's think."

"Well, you could find a man with money and get a quickie wedding on the Strip."

I laugh again, turning over onto my stomach. "At this point, that's the only way I'll get married—inebriated and to a stranger." *The guys I date aren't marriage material. I'll probably be alone forever at this rate.*

"Hey, people find love in all sorts of ways."

"True, but the odds that I'll find a marry-able man in the next few hours is incredibly low." I fold my arms under my head. "In lieu of sexy strangers with an engagement ring in their pocket, what else do you suggest?"

She taps a finger to her lips. "We could go to a show tonight. A male striptease or something like that. It might be a way to get your juices flowing—"

"Ew!"

"*While lacking permanence.* Then just see where the night takes us. Be free-spirited."

"You just want to go because it's one more way to needle Brock."

Her grin is full of mischief. "So? What's your point?"

Ella and my brother have been *a thing* for almost two years. *What kind of thing?* I'm afraid to label it, although I'm fairly certain they're exclusive without declaring exclusivity.

On the one hand, Ella is a lot to handle. She's smart, opinionated, and doesn't need a man—and she knows it. She also has a propensity to make decisions and weigh the risks after. That drives Brock nuts.

On the other hand, dating Brock would be a nightmare. Women throw themselves at him wherever he goes. Men stop him for autographs and to *man-swoon* over him. And during the season, he's focused and mostly unavailable. That doesn't always work for Ella.

I watch this back-and-forth and vow never to get into a relationship with a player—an athlete or otherwise. *Again.* I've done that before, and it didn't end well.

"I'm taking it you two are still fighting," I say.

"We aren't fighting. There's nothing to fight about." She lifts her chin to the sky. "I'm right, and he's wrong. That's all there is to it."

"I agree. You're right this time."

Her eyes widen. "*You're damn right I'm right.* I'm not putting up with him taking off to Miami with his friends and not even mentioning our anniversary."

"How can you have an anniversary if you aren't in an official relationship?" I snicker. "Isn't that what you always tell me? That you aren't in an official relationship with him?"

She waves a hand through the air, dismissing my question. "It's a prelationship, but that doesn't change anything in this circumstance."

"A *what?*"

"A *prelationship.* The formative stage where boundaries and expectations are established so you can determine if the other person is willing to abide by them." She pauses. "*Brock isn't.*"

I roll my eyes and let it go. They'll settle this before Brock returns from Miami and we're home from Vegas. I've seen it too many times to count.

"Then fine," I say, sitting up. "Let's go to a show. But if my brother asks whose idea it was, I'm not taking the blame."

"Tell him it was mine. *I want him to know.* A little competition never hurt anyone."

"Competition for your non-boyfriend?" I ask, grinning.

"Precisely."

I shake my head as a bead of sweat trickles down my face. I wipe it away with the back of my hand. "I'm ready to go in and grab a shower."

"And I need to make reservations for dinner." She sits up, slipping on her flip-flops. "You owe me, you know."

"What do I owe you for?"

"For depriving me of my right as your best friend to throw you the most outrageous, amazing birthday party that Nashville has ever seen." She stuffs her water bottle in her bag. "I'm known in certain circles as the girl who throws the best bashes. I can only wonder what everyone is thinking about this."

I laugh at her ridiculousness, slipping my cover-up over my head. "You've thrown me a huge birthday party every year I've known you. You can miss this one. It won't hurt."

She frowns. "Maybe it won't hurt *you*, but it pains *me*. I have a reputation to uphold."

"You'll survive."

I drop my phone, towel, and water bottle into my bag. I skim the area around me to ensure I have everything.

"Ready?" she asks.

"Yeah." A bubble of excitement fills me. *Let the birthday festivities commence.* "Let's go find trouble."

Ella shares my smile as we slide our bags on our sun-kissed shoulders. I spot my book under her chair and grab it. *How did it get there?*

As I stand, my gaze falls on Ella. Her wide eyes are twinkling. I've seen this look enough times to know things are about to get real.

"What?" I ask, frozen in place.

Her grin pulls wider. "I think trouble just found us."

Oh no.

Read more (and see more Landry Security heroes!) in The Proposal, available on Amazon and Audible.

Acknowledgments

Thank you to my Creator for all the blessings in my life.

All my love to my husband and sons for understanding what life looks like with a writer. I love you all so freaking much.

My bonus parents are the absolute best. Thank you for loving me and supporting this crazy job.

Thank you to Kari March for designing the perfect cover and to Michelle Lancaster for the perfect photograph.

Sending love to my friends for their support, laughs, and brainstorming sessions: Mandi Beck, S.L. Scott, Jessica Prince, Dylan Allen, Anjelica Grace, Kenna Rey, and Chelle Sloan.

I'm so thankful for the love and support of Michele Ficht and Brittni Van.

I can't say enough about my editors Marion Archer and Jenny Sims. Thank you for working me in. *winks*

As always, a huge thank you to the women who help me and my groups run smoothly—Tiffany Remy, Kaitie Reister, Stephanie Gibson, Jordan Fazzini, and Sue Maturo. I adore you all.

The team at Valentine PR is amazing. Thank you, everyone, for your patience and hard work. You are appreciated.

Thank you to the team in Books by Adriana Locke, led by the fearless Atlee, who have lobbied for years for Troy's book. What can I say? You won. I'm so grateful for your support and enthusiasm for my words. *hugs*

Last but certainly not least, thank you to my readers. I get to tell stories for a living because of you. I'm forever grateful.

About the Author

USA Today Bestselling author, Adriana Locke, writes contemporary romances about the two things she knows best—big families and small towns. Her stories are about ordinary people finding extraordinary love with the perfect combination of heart, heat, and humor.

She loves connecting with readers, fall weather, football, reading alpha heroes, everything pumpkin, and pretending to garden.

Hailing from a tiny town in the Midwest, Adriana spends her free time with her high school sweetheart (who she married over twenty years ago) and their four sons (who truly are her best work).

Her kitchen may be a perpetual disaster, and if all else fails, there is always pizza.

Join her reader group and talk all the bookish things by clicking here.

www.adrianalocke.com

Made in United States
Orlando, FL
03 June 2024

47507454R00127